Eva Mae,
  I hope you enjoy this volume of Wyoming short stories. Thank you for your friendship.

Wyoming Sun

Love,
Niki

Other Books by Edward Bryant

Among the Dead
Phoenix Without Ashes (with Harlan Ellison)
Cinnabar
2076: The American Tricentennial (editor, with Jo Ann Harper)
Particle Theory

Wyoming Sun

by
Edward Bryant

Photographs by
MICHAEL McCLURE

Introduction by
ROBERT RORIPAUGH

1980

JELM MOUNTAIN PRESS • LARAMIE

ACKNOWLEDGMENTS

"Prairie Sun," copyright © 1980 by Omni Publications International Ltd. Appeared originally in *Omni*.

"giANTS," copyright © 1979 by The Conde Nast Publications, Inc. Appeared originally in *Analog Science Fiction/Science Fact*.

"Teeth Marks," copyright © 1979 by Mercury Press, Inc. Appeared originally in *The Magazine of Fantasy and Science Fiction*.

"Beyond the Sand River Range," copyright © 1972 by Lancer Books, Inc. Appeared originally in *Infinity*.

"Strata," copyright © 1980 by Mercury Press, Inc. Appeared originally in *The Magazine of Fantasy and Science Fiction*.

Copyright © 1980 by Edward Bryant.

Illustrations copyright © 1980 by Michael McClure.

If I attempted to thank everyone whose generous aid went into this cooperative publishing venture and these stories, there would be little space left for the fiction. So thank you, friends. You know who you are.

Jo, thank you especially. This book would not have been...

Cover and jacket design by Phil Normand and Ad•Venture Graphics. Cover based upon original art by Scot Weir. Photograph of the author by R. Dewey Vanderhoff/Alpenglow Photo.

All rights reserved, including the right to reproduce this book or portions thereof in any form whatsoever. For information address:

Jelm Mountain Press
209 Grand Ave., Suite 205
Laramie, Wyoming 82070

Library of Congress Cataloging in Publication Data

Bryant, Edward, 1945-
   Wyoming sun.

  1. Wyoming—Fiction. 2. Science Fiction, American.
I. Title.
PZ4.B91484Wy [PS3552.R879]   813'.54   80-16646
ISBN 0-936204-15-X

FIRST JELM MOUNTAIN PRESS PRINTING OCTOBER 1980

Printed in the U.S.A.

*For Walter Edens
who saved me from the horrors
of Freshman English.*

Contents

Introduction 11

Prairie Sun 17

giANTS 33

Teeth Marks 57

Beyond the Sand River Range 81

Strata 93

Wyoming Sun

"I do not fear the future. I *do* fear the lazy utilization of Wyoming's future."
>
> —James Michener
> Laramie
> August 21, 1979

Introduction

Edward Bryant is a Wyoming writer. A native of the state who grew up in the Wheatland area and attended the University of Wyoming in the 1960's as an English major, he is also an author returning home imaginatively in the fiction collected in *Wyoming Sun*. Since completing his creative-writing M.A. at the University in 1968, Ed has become—through talent, originality, hard work, and tenacity—one of the state's most successful writers. Currently an editor (*2076: The American Tricentennial*), workshop instructor, winner of the Nebula Award from the Science Fiction Writers of America for the best short story of 1979, and author of two volumes of stories (*Among the Dead* and *Cinnabar*), a novel (*Phoenix Without Ashes*), and with two further books forthcoming (*Particle Theory* and *A Kingdom by the Sea*), Ed Bryant is nationally recognized as a fine science-fiction and fantasy writer whose future will be interesting to watch, but whose present accomplishments are already large.

This alone would make *Wyoming Sun* appealing to readers as a volume of fiction by an excellent craftsman. But other qualities are apparent in the stories collected here. For example, the concept of "place"—an involvement with a particular well-realized locale, which is important to many who write about a region—is evident throughout *Wyoming Sun,* whether the story's setting is the Oregon Trail near Douglas, Wind River Canyon, a small town like "Fremont" in the central part of the state, or a futuristic Casper that is both familiar and blurring into uneasy mutation. Bryant's stories are not nostalgic in their use of locale and authentic Wyoming backgrounds, and certainly not sentimental. He does, however, see the land—and nature itself—as possessing a brooding spirit which is in opposition to man's abuses, folly, and egotism . . . and capable of emerging into terrifying forms in such stories as "giANTS" and "Strata."

A second, sometimes related aspect of interest found in *Wyoming Sun* is the ethical/moral element which James Michener's epigraph touches upon. "Prairie Sun" is a story that considers values placed upon charity in 1850, during the immigration West, as they conflict with those of a sterile, regimented future. The treatment of the state's Native Americans is highlighted by an ironic turn of the screw in "Beyond the Sand River Range." And "Strata," in its revelation of conflict between environment and exploitation in Wyoming, is much more than what its author calls "a scientific ghost story," though it is that too. If speculative fiction provides images of where we might be heading, in Bryant's hands it can also question the ethical cost of getting there. And do so within the framework of entertaining storytelling.

Not surprisingly, then, we find ourselves responding to these fictional reflections of Wyoming as stories both intriguing and solidly written. Within them are people whose characters are explored in psychological depth, such as Frank

Introduction xiii

Alessi, in "Teeth Marks," who returns home to his destiny after a political career disintegrates, his whole life exposed mercilessly before the story's end. And Dr. Paul Chavez of "giANTS," who tells us that following the death of his wife, "I disengaged myself from most sectors of life" and "decided to hold onto the past and call it good," but is almost jarred into salvation by a young woman reporter. We can recognize the sound portrayals of Paul Onoda in "Strata," a Sansei survivor of Wyoming's Heart Mountain Relocation Center who drives himself toward success as an exploration geologist for an energy company, and the woman he marries, Carroll Dale, rooted to the land through several generations of ranchers.

Such figures take on complexity and interest in Bryant's writing, but characterization is complemented by skillful plotting in which resolutions of the conflicts are both jolting and subtle. Events are thrown into entirely new perspectives in "Beyond the Sand River Range," resolved into sharp, ironic symbolism in "giANTS" and "Strata," or into contemplative senses of horror and understanding in "Teeth Marks" and "Prairie Sun." The reader is surprised at times by plot, as he should be in stories that avoid predictability. To Bryant's credit, the plot turns also take us deeper into character and meaning, rather than creating contrived shock or titillation.

Ultimately we become impressed by the author's ability to make language convey not only what is happening with his characters and their actions, but also to influence our emotions and responses to what occurs. "Teeth Marks" and "giANTS" are perhaps the most obvious examples of language and style at work, but the other stories display similar control and effectiveness, though in differing ways.

Here then are stories involving Wyoming backgrounds and people which illuminate past, present and future . . . and what meanings they may hold when viewed by an intelligent, imaginative mind. They are stories both entertaining and written with skill, for Ed Bryant is a professional in his field whose work indicates that, in one sense or another, Wyoming's literary tomorrows could indeed be fantastic.

Robert Roripaugh
University of Wyoming

THIS FIRST story is set in 1850. A science fiction story taking place in nineteenth-century Wyoming? Well, why not? Just because the bulk of science fiction deals with the future doesn't decree that SF cannot concern itself as well with the past. Good science fiction, as with the best fiction of any variety, attempts to deal first and foremost with the love and hate, trust and betrayal, all the other personal ties between human beings that link us in any *era. Hard answers to genuine human problems are demanded of Micah, the boy—young man, rather—in "Prairie Sun," as he finds himself in decidedly curious circumstances on the plains east of Casper in the year 1850.*

"Prairie Sun" came about as a direct result of "Strata," the final story in the book. In June 1979 I attended the Wyoming Writers annual workshop, held that year in Riverton. Afterward, a friend and I drove up and down the Wind River Canyon, doing research and taking notes for "Strata." Then, driving toward Casper on U.S. 20-26, I saw a historical marker commemorating the Oregon Trail. I looked at that bleak stone and thought back to Mrs. Roberts' fifth-grade Wyoming history class. I remembered the lore of wagon trains trekking westward and something in my brain went click. *A few weeks later, I wrote this story.*

Prairie Sun

STILLNESS.

Except for the boy, nothing moved on the prairie. The hawks did not hunt this morning. Not even the vultures circled in the empty sky. The birds evidently were waiting until Micah Taverner made his kill.

The heat hung like a heavy curtain over the world. All motion seemed suspended. The thought entered Micah's mind that on these plains, anything at all could happen. His was a sudden and early maturity, and not one he relished.

Thirteen-year-old Micah moved quietly—perhaps not so silently as an Indian, but still disturbing the saw-toothed grass with less noise than most others in the company. He balanced his father's long muzzle-loader carefully, thumb ready to take the hammer off half-cock. A small antelope would be welcome. A young deer would be better. A rabbit would suffice.

To Micah's right the River Platte wound slowly east by south, the direction from which the company had come. At this point the road followed a straighter path than the river. The boy's present course took him up a gentle rise so that he had now attained an elevation of a hundred yards above the river. Within a rod of the Platte, all was lush and green. The grass and the trees grew luxuriantly. Beyond them the world turned to shades of brown and tan and yellow.

The world seemed to contain little more than the river and the prairie. And the road. Had he wished to stand in the ruts, they would have taken the boy in up to his waist.

Micah heard a sound in the dead air. He froze, waiting. He heard something again. Glass breaking. The mutter of words. The sounds came from beyond the low rise ahead. Two voices. Whoever were speaking, they were close by the trail.

The boy slowly cocked the hammer of the rifle. It seemed to him the click echoed out across the parched land like the gunshot itself. Again he heard words too distant and indistinct to understand. But the tone did not sound alarmed.

White men? he thought. *Pawnee!* had been the first word in his mind. Or Sioux. Or Blackfeet. He had heard the tales of slaughter and torture from the talkers around the fire. He had listened then with eyes wide and the breath catching in his throat, even though his father had laughed and suggested wryly that the red tribes were no more monsters than were the men of the company. And after all, men of other companies had given deadlier gifts than bullets to the Indians.

Micah gripped his father's rifle tighter and stealthily approached the summit. Sounds again—this time a rattle as though iron articles and wood were being placed together in a bag. Outcroppings of porous stone afforded the boy some cover as he reached the hill's crest.

White! At least the strangers were not red men, though they appeared odd to Micah's eyes. There were two of them, and they were poking through the heaps of discards beside the trail. The road was lined with all manner of belongings thrown away by the exhausted, overburdened men and women barely halfway along their arduous journey. The wagons, the oxen, the horses and mules, the people—all could carry only so much across the months and the thousands of miles demanded.

Micah had seen the jettisoned tools and household goods start to appear beside the wagon ruts not long after Fort Phil Kearney, many miles even before reaching the ford of the South Platte. Before the sickness began, his father had tried keeping a running tally of what he saw for just a mile or two. "There must be ten thousand dollars worth of goods there," he had said. "All for the picking had one the time or the desire."

But few struggling toward California or Oregon, of course, had the time or the desire. So the prized New England heirloom furniture, the discarded barrels of flour and sacks of white beans, the Franklin stoves and the printing presses, all lay rotting beneath the prairie sun.

And now Micah saw the two strange white men rooting like hogs among the once-prized belongings scattered beside the road. Their backs were to him, so for a while he watched without their knowledge. Both men were tall, each easily attaining a height of over six feet. Though one had dark hair and the other was a towhead with hair as light as the dried grass, they seemed much alike in appearance. The pair wore similar clothing: plaid shirts with braces, brown cloth trousers, and thick-soled boots. The towhead's shirt was red; the darker man's was green. But Micah saw there was something not quite right about the clothing. For one thing, the cloth was slick and it gleamed under the direct sun. For another, he abruptly realized as the men flexed to pick up objects that each man's outfit was all of one piece of material. It was as though each were wearing a set of long-johns colored to appear as real clothing.

The towhead was showing the other a New England hooked rug much like the treasure Micah's mother still packed deep in the wagon after adamantly refusing to discard it at the Platte River crossing. Micah wondered if he should accost them or if it would be wiser simply to backtrack along the trail and forage in another direction. Then the darker man turned slightly, glanced up, and looked straight at Micah. He said something to his companion. Both of them stared at the boy.

Finally one of them, the towhead, said, "Come on down here, young man." He put down the hooked rug and stood there quietly with empty hands. The other man slowly spread his hands, palms outward. Micah realized they were both looking at his father's muzzle-loader.

He warily approached the pair, then looked beyond them. The muzzle of the rifle came up. "Don't—" said the dark-haired man. Whatever else he was going to say was interrupted by the black-powder explosion. Two yards of decapitated prairie rattler jerked and flopped in death-throes close by their feet as each man yelled and leaped aside. They looked from the snake to Micah and back to the snake again.

"Thank you, boy," said the towhead.

"Mighty big one," said Micah. He felt very pleased with the shot and tried not to grin. He started to reload the rifle. "Probably the biggest one I've seen."

The men exchanged glances. "What's your name, son?" said the darker man.

Micah told them.

"Well now, Master Micah Taverner," said the towhead. "Please call me John. My friend here is Droos." Droos inclined his head. "We both of us truly do appreciate your eliminating the serpent."

"It wasn't nothing," Micah said as he rammed wadding down the barrel. "Just glad to help."

There was a silence. The men seemed trying to communicate with each other by sharp looks. Micah paid attention only to the muzzle-loader.

Finally John said, "I suppose you're wondering what the two of us are doing out here."

"None of my business," said Micah.

"Admirable," said Droos, turning away. "His mouth isn't as extraordinarily loose as yours, John. Now let's get back to work and see if we can find any more East Middlebury bottles like the one you so carelessly dropped."

But John seemed fascinated by the boy. "May I asked what *you're* doing out here?" he said. "I believe the last train passed by here nearly a week ago, and the next wagons aren't due for days."

"My mother sent me to look for game," said Micah. "She believes that meat broth will soothe Annie's innards."

"Who is Annie?"

"My little sister. She is sick with the smallpox."

Droos turned around from the wooden crates in which he was rummaging and stared. "Smallpox? We totally eradicated that more than a century ago."

"In *our* time," said John.

"Your time?" said Micah, confused now.

"Never mind," said John. "It's a long story. Where's your wagon?"

"That way." Micah pointed back along the river. "About three miles. We should have stayed in Fort Laramie, but Annie did not seem so ill then. The rest of the company said they would wait an extra day at Independence Rock. I fear by now they will have gone on."

"But your family stayed alone."

"Annie cries out when the wagon moves. She is too weak. My mother thought that the rest might help her."

"Your mother," said John. "What about your father?"

Micah stared at the ground. "He took ill and died of the cholera shortly before the crossing of the Platte."

"God almighty," said Droos.

"And so your mother and you have brought the wagon this far since?" said John.

The boy nodded. "Some of the men of the company helped us. But they had their own wagons, and their families. And many of them were weak with cholera."

"Unbelievable," Droos said. He unconsciously fondled a silver teapot.

"Now we have seen the elephant," said Micah.

Droos cocked an eyebrow. "Elephants? You actually found one here?"

Micah looked equally quizzical. "It means only that we found far more on our path than we expected. We would return to Ross County, Ohio, but it is now just as far to go back as it is to go on. Perhaps we can catch up with the company when Annie is better. Before he rode on, the captain told us we would have to move soon, or we should all be caught by the winter in the Sierra Nevada."

The two men stared at him, transfixed.

"People truly used to live and die this way," Droos said bemusedly.

"Micah," said John slowly. "Can you keep a secret?"

"If it is an honorable secret."

"What if I told you that we both were from the future?"

The boy shook his head. "I do not understand."

Droos opened his mouth as though to protest. John held up a restraining hand. "Droos and I are travelers, and we've come a great distance to be here. But we didn't make the sort of journey you might imagine. Not from England, not around the Horn; but instead, through time. What year is it, Micah?"

"The year of our Lord, 1850."

"Our world exists more than two centuries beyond that."

Micah shook his head silently. Food meant something. Sickness meant something. But the future? His mind already reeled with too many burdens.

John turned toward Droos, who was slowly stowing a silver tea service in a fabric pack. "Can you explain it more adequately?"

Droos stared down at the objects he held. "These are truly exquisite," he said. "Standish Barry, Baltimore, probably about 1820."

"*Droos.*"

The dark-haired man looked up and said, "This is against all the rules, you know. Why must you be a compulsive fool?"

"I was the only one in the department you could trust." John bent down to look at Micah levelly. "Do you know about the Romans?"

Micah nodded. "Father read us stories."

"Have you ever thought about what it would be like if you could really go back and visit the Romans?"

"Yes," said Micah.

"Well, we can do that, Micah. We live in your future. We can come back and visit your time, or the time of the Romans, or any other time of our choosing. We come from a year when smallpox has long since been banished from the Earth and most other diseases eliminated equally."

Micah knew he did not understand all that was being said to him. But a few words punched through the confusion. "You can heal smallpox?"

"Our ancestors did," said John. "Your grandchildren will."

"Can you cure Annie?"

Time again seemed suspended on the prairie. Everything was still. Micah stared at the men. They stared back at him.

"Well, I suppose . . ." said John.

"No," said Droos.

"Droos has an emergency medical kit; it might alleviate

the symptoms."

"No." This time Droos's answer was more vehement.

John wheeled angrily on his companion. "Just once," he said.

"Absolutely not," said Droos. "If I have to pull rank, I'll do so."

"One child," said John. "One life."

Droos dropped a dozen silver spoons and let them lie on the dusty trailside. "Let me remind you of a few things," he said. "I'm not being arbitrary about denying your humanitarian impulse. The first thing is that this is not exactly a sanctioned mission, you know. The second thing is that we'll be strung up doubly by our balls if the department finds out we've been salvaging collectibles from the past for resale in the present. Third, there's the primary travel directive—"

"Come *on*," said John. "Saving one little girl's life is highly unlikely to alter the future in any significant—"

Droos interrupted him, raising his voice even higher. "We don't *know* that. It's one thing to scavenge these antiques because nature would have destroyed them anyway. It's quite another to meddle with lives. Besides, we don't know that his sister is going to die of smallpox. She might recover. I believe children were more resilient—"

"I say we do it," said John.

"If I have to, I'll put your neck on the block without endangering mine," said Droos, his voice quiet and deadly. "I am capable of that, you know."

"I know that." John spread his arms helplessly. "Please?"

"No. There are rules—and these rules we will follow implicitly. We live in that kind of world." Droos knelt and began picking up the spoons, blowing the dust off and polishing them against his leg, before placing the utensils inside a bag of soft cloth. "Accept that."

In the ensuing silence, Micah said, "Can you cure Annie?"

John did not meet his eye this time. The towheaded man hesitated for a long time. Finally he said, "No, we can't. I'm sorry, Micah."

Micah considered that. Then he said, "But you could?"

Neither man said anything.

"But you won't?"

John flushed. Droos stowed the packet of silver and extracted a crystal loop-and-petal candlestick from a crate. "I'm truly sorry," said John. "I never should have spoken at all."

Very slowly, Micah said, "Father used to tell me, 'I help my friends; God help my enemies.' "

"We're not your enemies," said John earnestly. "There are simply rules that say we cannot be the friends we'd wish."

Micah said nothing. He only turned and, picking up both the dead snake and the muzzle-loader that leaned against a free-standing gilt mirror in its hardwood frame, walked away from the two men.

Micah distractedly shot the rabbit on the way back to the wagon. The big jack darted from the brush, and then made the mistake of pausing to assess the intruder on the plains. The ball passed cleanly through its right eye. The meat was unspoiled.

When the boy arrived at the wagon, the sun was long past its zenith. The oxen looked up incuriously to greet him, then bent their heavy heads back to the tough grass. Micah paused by the rear of the wagon.

"Ma?" he said. "I have a snake and a rabbit, Ma."

His mother drew the canvas flap aside and held a finger to her lips. "Hush," she said. "Your sister is dying." The gay colors of her gingham stood in stark contrast to the somber gray of the canvas top.

They waited an hour, then a second hour beside the small bed, listening to Annie's labored breathing. They took turns squeezing new compresses for the girl's forehead. Every few minutes, Micah took the bucket to the river for fresh, cold water.

Annie's face continued to shine with sweat, even with the compresses. At the same time, she shook as though with a chill, and they kept her bundled in her mother's hand-loomed blankets.

Finally the breathing stopped. Mother and brother waited minutes in the sudden stillness. Micah started to touch his mother's shoulder. She shook his hand aside. "Let me be alone," she said. Slowly she unwound the fine wool blankets and took up her daughter's body in her arms. Without words, she stepped down from the wagon and walked through the cottonwood and boxelder toward the river's edge.

Micah stood in the rear of the wagon and watched her go. The thought reverberated in his mind: what sort of people would allow a child to die this way? What form of Christian charity would let his sister perish in such a fashion?

He realized he simply did not know.

After what seemed a long, long time, Micah emptied his mother's most prized possession, the finely carved sandalwood chest, and repacked it.

The two men who claimed to be from the future were a half-mile further down the trail from where they had met with Micah. They were still rummaging through the heaps of abandoned goods, apparently working their way toward Missouri.

Scrub cottonwoods, sage, a dusty draw, juts of porous stone, the wagon ruts themselves, all lent Micah cover. The boy knew that an Indian would have discerned him in a moment. But John and Droos had no such skills. For the second time, but for only a moment, Micah truly wondered what it was like in the future. Then his mind told him once again that such speculation was an impossible luxury, and he bent all his effort to remaining undiscovered.

For two or three seconds he actually stood in full view had they only looked up. But both men were apparently absorbed in examining a bulky contraption of legs and drawers. Micah set the sandalwood chest down in the dust, strategically in sight only a few yards beyond the men. Then he melted back into the country's natural cover.

In a few minutes Micah reappeared, walking down the slope toward John and Droos and making no effort at concealment. The two men were looking over a William and Mary highboy, touching the smooth finish, sliding the drawers in and out, checking the joints. "Note the lacquered Chinese detail," said Droos. "Though not actually executed by Oriental artisans, the figures are Chinese in both feeling and technique." Buried in his task, he did not look up to see why John had not responded until Micah stood before them both.

The boy's face was coated with dust; his eyes felt like burnt holes in a mask. He tasted prairie grit and would have spat out the dirt, but he no longer had the saliva.

John sounded unsure and awkward. "Hello, Micah. Welcome back. We were just preparing to—leave. Our time is almost up."

Micah looked from one to the other steadily. He had to start the words several times because of the dry rasp in his throat. "You still would do nothing for my sister?"

"We *can* do nothing," said Droos. "We come from a quite different world, Micah. There are things we must not do. There are rules."

Micah turned his gaze to John. John finally stared at the ground and nodded agreement. "Very well," the boy said, sounding tired and much older than his thirteen years. The men looked at him warily.

"I truly am sorry," said John.

Micah said nothing. Nor did he answer any other entreaty made by either of the men. He retreated to sit on a wooden crate that held mining tools and simply watched them.

"We'd best get back to work," said Droos, checking something on his wrist. With redoubled energy, the two men again busied themselves among the debris. Every once in a while they looked at Micah. The boy remained stationary on the box.

"A swirl bottle!" said Droos. "A second!"

"This looks like a Pennsylvania Dutch door hanging," said John.

"A full set of eighteenth-century sextant gear."

"Another Roosevelt teapot."

"What's this?" John hunkered down beside the sandalwood chest.

"What extraordinary workmanship," said Droos, also bending over the chest. "Absolutely gorgeous." His fingertips ran eagerly over the inlaid panels. Then he raised the flat lid and said, "Oh yes, yes indeed." Drawing the contents from the chest, he said, "Shetland?"

"Looks like it," said John.

And loomed by my mother's hand, thought Micah, but spoke no word aloud.

Droos again inspected his wrist and said, "Damn! It's almost over. You attach a tracer to the chest. I'll finish up the rest."

Their departure was not dramatic.

"Ten seconds," said Droos, adjusting something at his belt.

John at least spoke to Micah. "Good-bye," he said, offering a slow, sad wave of his hand. "I'm sorry, Micah."

Both men simply were gone. As though they had never existed. Micah watched as all up and down the trail, objects vanished. Crates and bags melted into the air. The massive

William and Mary highboy disappeared. Finally his mother's sandalwood chest vanished too, and along with it, the fine hand-loomed blankets of good Shetland wool, the blankets that had kept his sister from the frontier cold these past nights.

Micah stood then, and hoped his mother was waiting for him at the wagon. The chest and blankets were gone. They had left him there to stand sweating in the prairie sun; in a plain of near-absolute stillness, hushed but no longer expectant; a plain on which, it seemed to him, anything at all could happen.

And it had.

MY UNCLE Earl took me to an incredible number of movies in the 1950's. I loved going to monster movies at the Ramona Theater in Wheatland. I especially liked giant bug flicks such as Them! *and* Tarantula. *So what if most were black and white and cheaply made? I still loved them. Even though I've presumably grown up and my tastes have changed, I keep a real nostalgia for clumsy matte shots of rampaging bugs destroying American cities. All that is in spite of moving away from Wyoming for quite a long time, hearing that the Ramona burned down in the 'sixties, and being disillusioned by Isaac Asimov telling me how impossible it is for insects the size of horses to exist.*

Actually the roots of "giANTS" probably go back to the summer afternoon on the ranch when my mother found me happily perched on a red ant hill, playing with the natives. I was not very old at the time, and am delighted to have survived to become older. Truth to tell, I don't feel this is a story about ants *so much as it is simply a people story in which ants are only supporting actors. Soon after "giANTS" was published, a Casper reporter read it, deduced I was an Old Wyoming Boy, and interviewed me by telephone. In the city edition of the* Star-Tribune, *the headline editor attached the lead, GIANT ANTS STALK THE CITY. Reporter John Wheaton, a genuinely conscientious journalist, immediately protested and the state edition carried the more austere (and accurate) lead, SF STORY SET IN CASPER. So it goes . . .*

giANTS

PAUL CHAVEZ LOOKED FROM THE CARD ON THE SILVER PLATE to O'Hanlon's face and back to the card. "I couldn't find the tray," she said. "Put the thing away maybe twelve years ago and didn't have time to look. Never expected to need it." Her smile folded like parchment and Chavez thought he heard her lips crackle.

He reached out and took the card. Neat black-on-white printing asserted that one Laynie Bridgewell was a bona fide correspondent from the UBC News Billings bureau. He turned the card over. Sloppy cursive script deciphered as: "Imperitive I talk to you about New Mexico Project."

"Children of electronic journalism," Chavez said amusedly. He set the card back on the plate. "I suppose I ought to see her in the drawing room—if I were going to see her, which I'm not."

"She's a rather insistent young woman," said O'Hanlon.

Chavez sat stiffly down on the couch. He plaited his fingers and rested the palms on the crown of his head. "It's surely time for my nap. Do be polite."

"Of course, Dr. Chavez," said O'Hanlon, sweeping silently out of the room, gracefully turning as she exited to close the doors of the library.

Pain simmered in the joints of his long bones. Chavez shook two capsules from his omnipresent pill case and poured a glass of water from the carafe on the walnut desk. Dr. Hansen had said it would only get worse. Chavez lay on his side on the couch and felt weary—seventy-two years' weary. He supposed he should have walked down the hall to his bedroom, but there was no need. He slept better here in the library. The hardwood panels and the subdued Mondrian originals soothed him. Endless ranks of books stood vigil. He loved to watch the wind-blown patterns of the pine boughs beyond the French windows that opened onto the balcony. He loved to study the colors as sunlight spilled through the leaded DNA double-helix pane Annie had given him three decades before.

Chavez felt the capsules working faster than he had expected. He thought he heard the tap of something hard against the glass. But then he was asleep.

In its basics, the dream never changed.

They were there in the desert somewhere between Albuquerque and Alamogordo, all of them: Ben Peterson, the tough cop; the FBI man Robert Graham; Chavez himself; and Patricia Chavez, his beautiful, brainy daughter.

The wind, gusting all afternoon, had picked up; it whistled steadily, atonally, obscuring conversation. Sand sprayed abrasively against their faces. Even the gaunt stands of spiny cholla bowed with the wind.

Patricia had struck off on her own tangent. She struggled up the base of a twenty-foot dune. She began to slip back almost as far as each step advanced her.

They all heard it above the wind—the shrill, ululating chitter.

"What the hell is that?" Graham yelled.

Chavez shook his head. He began to run toward Patricia. The sand, the wind, securing the brim of his hat with one hand: all conspired to make his gait clumsy.

The immense antennae rose first above the crest of the dune. For a second, Chavez thought they surely must be branches of wind-blown cholla. Then the head itself heaved into view, faceted eyes coruscating with changing hues of red and blue. Mandibles larger than a farmer's scythes clicked and clashed. The ant paused, apparently surveying the creatures downslope.

"Look at the size of it," said Chavez, more to himself than to the others.

He heard Peterson's shout. "It's as big as a horse!" He glanced back and saw the policeman running for the car.

Graham's reflexes were almost as prompt. He had pulled his .38 Special from the shoulder holster and swung his arm, motioning Patricia to safety, yelling, "Back, get back!" Patricia began to run from the dune all too slowly, feet slipping on the sand, legs constricted by the ankle-length khaki skirt. Graham fired again and again, the gun popping dully in the wind.

The ant hesitated only a few seconds longer. The wind sleeked the tufted hair on its purplish green thorax. Then it launched itself down the slope, all six articulated legs churning with awful precision.

Chavez stood momentarily frozen. He heard a coughing stutter from beside his shoulder. Ben Peterson had retrieved a Thompson submachine gun from the auto. Gouts of sand erupted around the advancing ant. The creature never hesitated.

Patricia lost her race in a dozen steps. She screamed once as the crushing mandibles closed around her waist. She looked despairingly at her father. Blood ran from both corners of her mouth.

There was an instant eerie tableau. The Tommy gun fell silent as Peterson let the muzzle fall in disbelief. The hammer of Graham's pistol clicked on a spent cylinder. Chavez cried out.

Uncannily, brutally graceful, the ant wheeled and, still carrying Patricia's body, climbed the slope. It crested the dune and vanished. Its chittering cry remained a moment more before raveling in the wind.

Sand flayed his face as Chavez called out his daughter's name over and over. Someone took his shoulder and shook him, telling him to stop it, to wake up. It wasn't Peterson or Graham.

It was his daughter.

She was his might-have-been daughter.

Concerned expression on her sharp-featured face, she was shaking him by the shoulder. Her eyes were dark brown and enormous. Her hair, straight and cut short, was a lighter brown.

She backed away from him and sat in his worn, leather-covered chair. He saw she was tall and very thin. For a moment he oscillated between dream-orientation and wakefulness. "Patricia?" Chavez said.

She did not answer.

Chavez let his legs slide off the couch and shakily sat up. "Who in the world are you?"

"My name's Laynie Bridgewell," said the young woman.

Chavez's mind focused. "Ah, the reporter."

"Correspondent."

"A semantic distinction. No essential difference." One level of his mind noted with amusement that he was articulating well through the confusion. He still didn't know what the hell was going on. He yawned deeply, stretched until a dart of pain cut the movement short, said, "Did you talk Ms. O'Hanlon into letting you up here?"

"Are you kidding?" Bridgewell smiled. "She must be a great watchdog."

"She's known me a long while. How *did* you get up here?"

Bridgewell looked mildly uncomfortable. "I, uh, climbed up."

"Climbed?"

"Up one of the pines. I shinnied up a tree to the balcony. The French doors were unlocked. I saw you inside sleeping, so I came in and waited."

"A criminal offense," said Chavez.

"They were unlocked," she said defensively.

"I meant sitting and watching me sleep. Terrible invasion of privacy. A person could get awfully upset, not knowing if another human being, a strange one at that, is secretly watching him snore or drool or whatever."

"You slept very quietly," said Bridgewell. "Very still. Until the nightmare."

"Ah," said Chavez. "It was that apparent?"

She nodded. "You seemed really upset. I thought maybe I ought to wake you."

Chavez said, "Did I say anything?"

She paused and thought. "Only two words I could make out. A name—Patricia. And you kept saying 'them.'"

"That figures." He smiled. He felt orientation settling around him like familiar wallpaper in a bedroom, or old friends clustering at a departmental cocktail party. "You're from the UBC bureau in Billings?"

"I drove down this morning."

"Work for them long?"

"Almost a year."

"First job?"

She nodded. "First real job."

"You're what—twenty-one?" said Chavez.

"Twenty-two."

"Native?"

"Of Montana?" She shook her head. "Kansas."

"University of Southern California?"

Another shake. "Missouri."

"Ah," he said. "Good school." Chavez paused. "You're here on assignment?"

A third shake. "My own time."

"Ah," said Chavez again. "Ambitious. And you want to talk to me about the New Mexico Project?"

Face professionally sober, voice eager, she said, "Very much. I didn't have any idea you lived so close until I read the alumni bulletin from the University of Wyoming."

"I wondered how you found me out." Chavez sighed. "Betrayed by my alma mater . . ." He looked at her sharply. "I don't grant interviews, even if I occasionally conduct them." He stood and smiled. "Will you be wanting to use the stairs, or would you rather shinny back down the tree?"

"Who is Patricia?" said Bridgewell.

"My daughter," Chavez started to say. "Someone from my past," he said.

"I lost people to the bugs," said Bridgewell quietly. "My parents were in Biloxi at the wrong time. Bees never touched them. The insecticide offensive got them both."

The pain in Chavez's joints became ice needles. He stood—and stared.

Even more quietly, Bridgewell said, "You don't have a daughter. Never had. I did my homework." Her dark eyes seemed even larger. "I don't know everything about the New Mexico Project—that's why I'm here. But I can stitch the rumors together." She paused. "I even had the bureau rent an old print of the movie. I watched it four times yesterday."

Chavez felt the disorientation return, felt exhausted, felt—damn it!—old. He fumbled the container of pain pills out of his trouser pocket, then returned it unopened. "Hungry?" he said.

"You better believe it. I had to leave before breakfast."

"I think we'll get some lunch," said Chavez. "Let's go downtown. Try not to startle Ms. O'Hanlon as we leave."

O'Hanlon had encountered them in the downstairs hall, but reacted only with a poker face. "Would you and the young lady like some lunch, Dr. Chavez?"

"Not today," said Chavez, "but thank you. Ms. Bridgewell and I are going to eat in town."

O'Hanlon regarded him. "Have you got your medicine?"

Chavez patted his trouser leg and nodded.

"And you'll be back before dark?"

"Yes," he said. "Yes. And if I'm not, I'll phone. You're not my mother. I'm older than you."

"Don't be cranky," she said. "Have a pleasant time."

Bridgewell and Chavez paused in front of the old stone house. "Why don't we take my car?" said Bridgewell. "I'll run you back after lunch." She glanced at him. "You're not upset about being driven around by a kid, are you?" He smiled and shook his head. "Okay."

They walked a hundred meters to where her car was pulled off the blacktop and hidden in a stand of spruce. It was a Volkswagen beetle of a vintage Chavez estimated to be a little older than its driver.

As if reading his thoughts, Bridgewell said, "Runs like a watch—the old kind, with hands. Got a hundred and ten thousand on her third engine. I call her Scarlett." The car's color was a dim red like dried clay.

"Do you really miss watches with hands?" said Chavez, opening the passenger-side door.

"I don't know—I guess I hadn't really thought about it. I know I don't miss slide-rules."

"*I* miss hands on timepieces." Chavez noticed there were no seatbelts. "A long time ago, I stockpiled all the Timexes I'd need for my lifetime."

"Does it really make any difference?"

"I suppose not." Chavez considered that as Bridgewell drove onto the highway and turned downhill.

"You love the past a lot, don't you?"

"I'm nostalgic," said Chavez.

"I think it goes a lot deeper than that." Bridgewell handled the VW like a racing Porsche. Chavez held onto the bar screwed onto the glove-box door with both hands. Balding radial tires shrieked as she shot the last curve and they began to descend the slope into Casper. To the east, across the city, they could see a ponderous dirigible-freighter settling gracefully toward a complex of blocks and domes.

"Why," she said, "are they putting a pilot fusion plant squarely in the middle of the biggest coal deposits in the country?"

Chavez shrugged. "When man entered the atomic age he opened a door into a new world. What he may eventually find in that new world no one can predict."

"Huh?" Bridgewell said. Then: "Oh, the movie. Doesn't it ever worry you—having that obsession?"

"No," said Chavez. Bridgewell slowed slightly as the road became city street angling past blocks of crumbling budget housing. "Turn left on Rosa. Head downtown."

"Where are we eating? I'm hungry enough to eat coal by-products."

"Close. We're going to the oil can."

"Huh?" Bridgewell said again.

"The Petroleum Tower. Over there." Chavez pointed at a forty-story cylindrical pile. It was windowed completely with bronze reflective panes. "The rooftop restaurant's rather good."

They left Scarlett in an underground lot and took the high-speed exterior elevator to the top of the Petroleum Tower. Bridgewell closed her eyes as the ground level rushed away from them. At the fortieth floor she opened her eyes to stare at the glassed-in restaurant, the lush hanging plants, the noontime crowd. "Who *are* these people? They all look so, uh, professional."

"They are that," said Chavez, leading the way to the maître d'. "Oil people. Uranium people. Coal people. Slurry people. Shale people. Coal gasification—"

"I've got the point," Bridgewell said. "I feel a little underdressed."

"They know me."

And so, apparently, they did. The maître d' issued orders and Bridgewell and Chavez were instantly ushered to a table beside a floor-to-ceiling window.

"Is this a perk of being maybe the world's greatest molecular biologist?"

Chavez shook his head. "More a condition of originally being a local boy. Even with the energy companies, this is still a small town at heart." He fell silent and looked out the window. The horizon was much closer than he remembered from his childhood. A skiff of brown haze lay over the city. There was little open land to be seen.

They ordered drinks.
They made small talk.
They ordered food.

"This is very pleasant," said Bridgewell, "but I'm still a correspondent. I think you're sitting on the biggest story of the decade."

"That extraterrestrial ambassadors are shortly to land near Albuquerque? That they have picked America as a way-station to repair their ship?"

Bridgewell looked bemused. "I'm realizing I don't know when you're kidding."

"Am I now?"

"Yes."

"So why do you persist in questioning me?"

She hesitated. "Because I suspect you want to tell someone. It might as well be me."

He thought about that awhile. The waiter brought the garnish tray and Chavez chewed on a stick of carrot. "Why don't you tell me the pieces you've picked up?"

"And then?"

"We'll see," he said. "I can't promise anything."

Bridgewell said, "You're a lot like my father. I never knew when he was kidding either."

"Your turn," said Chavez.

The soup arrived. Bridgewell sipped a spoonful of French onion and set the utensil down. "The New Mexico Project. It doesn't seem to have anything to do with New Mexico. You wouldn't believe the time I've spent on the phone. All my vacation I ran around that state in Scarlett."

Chavez smiled a long time, finally said, "Think metaphorically. The Manhattan Project was conducted under Stagg Field in Chicago."

"I don't think the New Mexico Project has anything to do with nuclear energy," she said. "But I have heard a lot of mumbling about DNA chimeras."

"So far as I know, no genetic engineer is using recombinant DNA to hybridize creatures with all the more loathesome aspects of snakes, goats, and lions. The state of the art improves, but we're not that good yet."

"But I shouldn't rule out DNA engineering?" she said.

"Keep going."

"Portuguese is the official language of Brazil."

Chavez nodded.

"UBC's stringer in Recife has it that, for quite a while now, nothing's been coming out of the Brazilian nuclear power complex at Xique-Xique. I mean there's *news,* but it's all through official release. Nobody's going in or out."

Chavez said, "You would expect a station that new and large to be a concern of national security. Shaking down's a long and complex process."

"Maybe." She picked the ripe olives out of the newly arrived salad and carefully placed them in a line on the plate. "I've got a cousin in movie distribution. Just real scutwork so far, but she knows what's going on in the industry. She told me that the U.S. Department of Agriculture ordered a print from Warner Bros. dubbed in Portuguese and had it shipped to Brasilia. The print was that movie you're apparently so concerned with—*Them!* The one about the ants mutating from radioactivity in the New Mexico desert. The one about giant ants on the rampage."

"Only a paranoid could love this chain of logic," said Chavez.

Her face looked very serious. "If it takes a paranoid to come up with this story and verify it," she said, "then that's what I am. Maybe nobody else is willing to make the jumps. I am. I know nobody else has the facts. I'm going to get them."

To Chavez, it seemed that the table had widened. He looked across the linen wasteland at her. "The formidable Formicidae family . . ." he said. "So have you got a conclussion to state?" He felt the touch of tiny legs on his leg. He felt feathery antennae tickle the hairs on his thigh. He jerked back from the table and his water goblet overturned, the waterstain spreading smoothly toward the woman.

"What's wrong?" said Bridgewell. He heard concern in

her voice. He slapped at his leg, stopped the motion, drew a deep breath.

"Nothing." Chavez hitched his chair closer to the table again. A waiter hovered at his shoulder, mopping the water with a towel and refilling the goblet. "Your conclusion." His voice strengthened. "I asked about your theory."

"I know this sounds crazy," said Bridgewell. "I've read about how the Argentine fire ants got to Mobile, Alabama. And I damned well know about the bees—I told you that."

Chavez felt the touch again, this time on his ankle. He tried unobtrusively to scratch and felt nothing. Just the touch. Just the tickling, chitinous touch.

"Okay," Bridgewell continued. "All I can conclude is that somebody in South America's created some giant, mutant ants, and now they're marching north. Like the fire ants. Like the bees."

"Excuse me a moment," said Chavez, standing.

"Your face is white," said Bridgewell. "Can I help you?"

"No." Chavez turned and, forcing himself not to run, walked to the restroom. In a stall, he lowered his trousers. As he had suspected, there was no creature on his leg. He sat on the toilet and scratched his skinny legs until the skin reddened and he felt the pain. "Damn it," he said to himself. "Stop." He took a pill from the case and downed it with water from the row of faucets. Then he stared at himself in the mirror and returned to the table.

"You okay?" Bridgewell had not touched her food.

He nodded. "I'm prey to any number of ailments; goes with the territory. I'm sorry to disturb your lunch."

"I'm apparently disturbing yours more."

"I offered." He picked up knife and fork and began cutting a slice of cold roast beef. "I offered—so follow this through. Please."

Her voice softened. "I have the feeling this all ties together somehow with your wife."

Chavez chewed the beef, swallowed without tasting it. "Did you look at the window?" Bridgewell looked blank. "The stained glass in the library."

Her expression became mobile. "The spiral design? The double helix? I loved it. The colors are incredible."

"It's exquisite; and it's my past." He took a long breath. "Annie gave it to me for my forty-first birthday. As well, it was our first anniversary. Additionally it was on the occasion of the award. It meant more to me than the trip to Stockholm." He looked at her sharply. "You said you did your homework. How much *do* you know?"

"I know that you married late," said Bridgewell, "for your times."

"Forty."

"I know that your wife died of a freak accident two years later. I didn't follow up."

"You should have," said Chavez. "Annie and I had gone on a picnic in the Florida panhandle. We were driving from Memphis to Tampa. I was cleaning some catfish. Annie wandered off, cataloguing insects and plants. She was an amateur taxonomist. For whatever reason—God only knows— I don't—she disturbed a mound of fire ants. They swarmed over her. I heard her screaming. I ran to her and dragged her away and brushed off the ants. Neither of us had known about her protein allergy—she'd just been lucky enough never to have been bitten or stung." He hesitated and shook his head. "I got her to Pensacola. Annie died in anaphylactic shock. The passages swelled, closed off. She suffocated in the car."

Bridgewell looked stricken. She started to say, "I'm sorry, Dr. Chavez, I had no—"

He held up his hand gently. "Annie was eight months pregnant. In the hospital they tried to save our daughter. It didn't work." He shook his head again, as if clearing it. "You and Annie look a bit alike—coltish, I think is the word. I expect Patricia would have looked the same."

The table narrowed. Bridgewell put her hand across the distance and touched his fingers. "You never remarried."

"I disengaged myself from most sectors of life." His voice was dispassionate.

"Why didn't you re-engage?"

He realized he had turned his hand over, was allowing his fingers to curl gently around hers. The sensation was warmth. "I spent the first half of my life single-mindedly pursuing certain goals. It took an enormous investment of myself to open my life to Annie." As he had earlier in the morning when he'd first met Bridgewell, he felt profoundly weary. "I suppose I decided to take the easier course: to hold onto the past and call it good."

She squeezed his hand. "I won't ask if it's been worth it."

"What about you?" he said. "You seem to be in ferocious pursuit of your goals. Do you have a rest of your life hidden off to the side?"

Bridgewell hesitated. "No. Not yet. I've kept my life directed, very concentrated, since—since everyone died. But someday . . ." Her voice trailed off. "I still have time."

"Time," Chavez said, recognizing the sardonicism. "Don't count on it."

Her voice very serious, she said, "Whatever happens, I won't let the past dictate to me."

He felt her fingers tighten. "Never lecture someone three times your age," he said. "It's tough to be convincing." He laughed and banished the tension.

"This *is* supposed to be an interview," she said, but didn't take her hand away.

"Did you ever have an ant farm as a child?" Chavez said. She shook her head. "Then we're going to go see one this afternoon." He glanced at the food still in front of her. "Done?" She nodded. "Then let's go out to the university field station."

They stood close together in the elevator. Bridgewell kept her back to the panoramic view. Chavez said, "I've given you no unequivocal statements about the New Mexico Project."

"I know."

"And if I should tell you now that there are indeed monstrous ant mutations—creatures large as horses—tramping toward us from the Mata Grosso?"

This time she grinned and shook her head silently.

"You think me mad, don't you?"

"I still don't know when you're kidding," she said.

"There are no giant ants," said Chavez. "Yet." And he refused to elaborate.

The field station of the Wyoming State University at Casper was thirty kilometers south, toward the industrial complex at Douglas-River Bend. Two kilometers off the freeway, Scarlett clattered and protested across the potholed access road, but delivered them safely. They crossed the final rise and descended toward the white dome and the cluster of outbuildings.

"That's huge," said Bridgewell. "Freestanding?"

"Supported by internal pressure," said Chavez. "We needed something that could be erected quickly. It was necessary that we have a thoroughly controllable internal environment. It'll be hell to protect from the snow and wind come winter, but we shouldn't need it by then."

There were two security checkpoints with uniformed guards. Armed men and women dubiously inspected the battered VW and its passengers, but waved them through when Chavez produced his identification.

"This is incredible," said Bridgewell.

"It wasn't my idea," said Chavez. "Rules."

She parked Scarlett beside a slab-sided building that adjoined the dome. Chavez guided her inside, past another checkpoint in the lobby, past obsequious underlings in lab garb who said, "Good afternoon, Dr. Chavez," and into a sterile-appearing room lined with electronic gear.

Chavez gestured at the rows of monitor screens. "We can't go into the dome today, but the entire installation is under surveillance through remotely controlled cameras." He began flipping switches. A dozen screens jumped to life in living color.

"It's all jungle," Bridgewell said.

"Rain forest." The cameras panned past vividly green trees, creepers, seemingly impenetrable undergrowth. "It's a reasonable duplication of the Brazilian interior. Now, listen." He touched other switches.

At first the speakers seemed to be crackling with electronic noise. "What am I hearing?" she finally said.

"What does it sound like?"

She listened longer. "Eating?" She shivered. "It's like a thousand mouths eating."

"Many more," Chavez said. "But you have the idea. Now watch."

The camera eye of the set directly in front of her dollied in toward a wall of greenery wound round a tree. Chavez saw the leaves ripple, undulating smoothly as though they were the surface of an uneasy sea. He glanced at Bridgewell; she saw it too. "Is there wind in the dome?"

"No," he said.

The view moved in for a closeup. "Jesus!" said Bridgewell.

Ants. Ants covered the tree, the undergrowth, the festooned vines.

"You may have trouble with the scale," Chavez said. "They're about as big as your thumb."

The ants swarmed in efficient concert, mandibles snipping like garden shears, stripping everything green, everything alive. Chavez stared at them and felt only a little hate. Most of the emotion had long since been burned from him.

"Behold *Eciton*," said Chavez. "Driver ants, army ants, the *maripunta*, whatever label you'd like to assign."

"I've read about them," said Bridgewell. "I've seen documentaries and movies at one time or another. I never thought they'd be this frightening when they were next door."

"There is fauna in the environment too. Would you like to see a more elaborate meal?"

"I'll pass."

Chavez watched the leaves ripple and vanish, bit by bit. Then he felt the tentative touch, the scurrying of segmented legs along his limbs. He reached out and tripped a single switch; all the pictures flickered and vanished. The two of them sat staring at the opaque gray monitors.

"Those are the giant ants?" she finally said.

"I told you the truth." He shook his head. "Not yet."

"No kidding now," she said.

"The following is a deliberate breach of national security," he said, "so they tell me." He raised his hands. "So what?" Chavez motioned toward the screens. "The *maripunta* apparently are mutating into a radically different form. It's not an obvious physical change, not like in *Them!* It's not by deliberate human agency, as with the bees. It may be through accidental human action—the Brazilian double-X nuclear station is suspected. We just don't know. What we do understand is that certain internal regulators in the *maripunta* have gone crazy."

"And they're getting bigger?" She looked bewildered.

He shook his head violently. "Do you know the square-cube law? No? It's a simple rule of nature. If an insect's dimensions are doubled, its strength and the area of its breathing passages are increased by a factor of four. But the mass is multiplied by eight. After a certain point, and that point isn't very high, the insect can't move or breathe. It collapses under its own mass."

"No giant ants?" she said.

"Not yet. Not exactly. The defective mechanism in the *maripunta* is one which controls the feeding and foraging phases. Ordinarily the ants—all the millions of them in a group—spend about two weeks in a nomadic phase. Then they alternate three weeks in place in a statary phase. That's how it used to be. Now only the nomadic phase remains."

"So they're moving," said Bridgewell. "North?" She sat with hands on knees. Her fingers moved as though with independent life.

"The *maripunta* are ravenous, breeding insanely, and headed our way. The fear is that, like the bees, the ants won't proceed linearly. Maybe they'll leapfrog aboard a charter aircraft. Maybe on a Honduran freighter. It's inevitable."

Bridgewell clasped her hands; forced them to remain still in her lap.

Chavez continued, "Thanks to slipshod internal Brazilian practices over the last few decades, the *maripunta* are resistant to every insecticide we've tried."

"They're unstoppable?" Bridgewell said.

"That's about it," said Chavez.

"And that's why the public's been kept in the dark?"

"Only partially. The other part is that we've found an answer." Chavez toyed with the monitor switches but stopped short of activating them. "The government agencies involved with this project fear that the public will misunderstand our solution to the problem. Next year's an election year." Chaves smiled ruefully. "There's a precedence to politics."

Bridgewell glanced from the controls to his face. "You're part of the solution. How?"

Chavez decisively flipped a switch and they again saw the ant-ravaged tree. The limbs were perceptibly barer. He left the sound down. "You know my background. You were correct in suspecting the New Mexico Project had something to do with recombinant DNA and genetic engineering. You're a good journalist. You were essentially right all down the line." He looked away from her toward the screen. "I and my people here are creating giant ants."

Bridgewell's mouth dropped open slightly. "I—but, you—"

"Let me continue. The purpose of the New Mexico Project has been to tinker with the genetic makeup of the *maripunta*— to create a virus-borne mutagen that will single out the queens. We've got that agent now."

All correspondent again, Bridgewell said, "What will it do?"

"At first we were attempting to readjust the ants' biological clocks and alter the nomadic phase. Didn't work; too sophisticated for what we can accomplish. So we settled for something more basic, more physical. We've altered the ants to make them huge."

"Like in *Them!*"

"Except that *Them!* was a metaphor. It stated a physical impossibility. Remember the square-cube law?" She nodded. "Sometime in the near future, bombers will be dropping payloads all across Brazil, Venezuela, the Guianas . . . anywhere we suspect the ants are. The weapon is dispersal bombs, aerosol cannisters containing the viral mutagen to trigger uncontrolled growth in each new generation of ants."

"The square-cube law . . ." said Bridgewell softly.

"Exactly. We've created monsters—and gravity will kill them."

"It'll work?"

"It should." Then Chavez said very quietly, "I hope I live long enough to see the repercussions."

Bridgewell said equally quietly, "I *will* file this story."

"I know that."

"Will it get you into trouble?"

"Probably nothing I can't handle." Chavez shrugged. "Look around you at this multi-million dollar installation. There were many more convenient places to erect it. I demanded it be built here." His smile was only a flicker. "When you're a giant in your field—and needed—the people in power tend to indulge you."

"Thank you, Dr. Chavez," she said.

"Dr. Chavez? After all this, it's still not Paul?"

"Thanks, Paul."

They drove north, back toward Casper, and watched the western photochemical sunset. The sun sank through the clouds in a splendor of reds. They talked very little. Chavez found the silence comfortable.

Why didn't you re-engage?

The question no longer disturbed him. He hadn't truly addressed it. Yet it was no longer swept under the carpet. That made all the difference.

I'll get to it, he thought. Chavez stared into the windshield sun-glare and saw his life bound up in a leaded pane like an ambered insect.

Bridgewell kept glancing at him silently as she drove up the long mountain road to Chavez's house. She passed the stand of pine where she had hidden Scarlett earlier in the day and braked to a stop in front of the stone house. They each sat still for the moment.

"You'll want to be filing your story," said Chavez.

She nodded.

"Now that you know the way up my tree, perhaps you'll return to visit in a more conventional way?"

Bridgewell smiled. She leaned across the seat and kissed

him on the lips. It was, Chavez thought, a more than filial kiss. "Now *I'm* not kidding," she said.

Chavez got out of the Volkswagen and stood on the flagstone walk while Bridgewell backed Scarlett into the drive and turned around. As she started down the mountain, she turned and waved. Chavez waved. He stood there and watched until the car vanished around the first turn.

He walked back to the house and found O'Hanlon waiting, arms folded against the twilight chill, on the stone step. Chavez hesitated beside her and they both looked down the drive and beyond. Casper's lights began to blossom into a growing constellation.

"Does she remind you considerably of what Patricia might have been like?" said O'Hanlon.

Chavez nodded, and then said quickly, "Don't go for easy Freud. There's more to it than that—or there may be."

A slight smile tugged at O'Hanlon's lips. "Did I say anything?"

"Well, no." Chavez stared down at the city. He said, with an attempt at great dignity, "We simply found out, in a short time, that we liked each other very much."

"I thought that might be it." O'Hanlon smiled a genuine smile. "Shall we go inside? Much longer out here and we'll be ice. I'll fix some chocolate."

He reached for the door. "With brandy?"

"All right."

"And you'll join me?"

"You know I ordinarily abstain, Dr. Chavez, but—" Her smile impossibly continued. "It is rather a special day, isn't it?" She preceded him through the warm doorway.

Chavez followed with a final look at the city. Below the mountain, Casper's constellation winked and bloomed into the zodiac.

Twelve hours later, the copyrighted story by Laynie Bridgewell made the national news and the wire services.

Eighteen hours later, her story was denied by at least five governmental agencies of two sovereign nations.

Twelve days later, Paul Chavez died quietly in his sleep, napping in the library.

Twenty-two days later, squadrons of jet bombers dropped cargoes of hissing aerosol bombs over a third of the South American continent. The world was saved. For a while, anyway. The grotesquely enlarged bodies of *Eciton burchelli* would shortly litter the laterite tropical soil.

Twenty-seven days later, at night, an intruder climbed up to the balcony of Paul Chavez's house on Casper Mountain and smashed the stained glass picture in the French doors leading into the library. No item was stolen. Only the window was destroyed.

"TEETH MARKS" is the story of a man's homecoming to the state which gave him birth and upbringing. When I attended Wheatland High School in the late 'fifties and early 'sixties, it was conventional wisdom that almost every young person who had anything on the ball would move out of Wyoming and find a career elsewhere. That tacit assumption that the Rocky Mountain West holds little future has been challenged with the advent of the energy boom. As the 'seventies wound down, I noted that more and more daughters and sons of the west either never left at all, or started coming back from Michigan and New York and California and wherever else they had scattered. Whether in the arts or business or industry, there are exciting futures for Wyoming's prodigal children. But some homecomings will not necessarily be pleasant . . .

Teeth Marks

My favorite vantage has always been the circular window at the end of the playroom. It is cut from the old-fashioned glass installed by Frank Alessi's father. As a young man, he built this house with his own hands. The slight distortions in the pane create a rainbow sheen when the light is proper. I enjoy the view so much more than those seen through the standard rectangular windows on the other floors, the panes regularly smashed by the enthusiasms of the young Alessis through the years and duly replaced. The circular window is set halfway between the hardwood floor and the peak of the gabled ceiling, low enough that I can watch the outside world from a chair.

Watching window scenes with slight distortions and enhanced colors satisfies my need for stimulation, since I don't read, nor go out to films, nor do I ever turn on the cold television console in the study. Sometimes I see jays quarreling with magpies, robins descending for meals on the unkempt lawn, ducks in the autumn and spring. I see the clouds form and roil through a series of shapes. The scene is hardly static, though it might seem such to a less patient observer. Patience must be my most obvious virtue, fixed here as I am on this eternal cutting edge of the present.

I possess my minor powers, but complete foreknowledge is not numbered among them. Long since taking up residence here, I've explored the dimensions of the house. Now I spend the bulk of my time in what I consider the most comfortable room in the house. I haunt the old-fashioned circular window, and I wait.

Frank Alessi took a certain bitter pleasure in driving his own car. All the years he'd had a staff and driver, he had forgotten the autonomous freedoms of the road. The feel of the wheel in his hands was a little heady. Any time he wanted, any time at all, he could twist the steering wheel a few degrees and direct the Ford into the path of a Trailways bus or a logging truck. It was his decision, reaffirmed from minute to minute on the winding mountain highway, his alone. He glanced at the girl beside him, not hearing what she was saying. She wouldn't be smiling so animatedly if she knew he was chilling his mind with an image of impalement on a bridge railing.

Her name was Sally Lakey, and he couldn't help thinking of her as a girl even though she'd told him at least three times that she had celebrated her twentieth birthday the week before.

"... *that* Alessi?" she said.

He nodded and half smiled.

"Yeah, really?" She cocked her head like some tropical bird and stared from large dark eyes.

Alessi nodded again and didn't smile.

"That's really something. Yeah, I recognize you from the

papers now. You're you." She giggled. "I even saw you last spring. In the campaign."

"The campaign," he repeated.

Lakey said apologetically, "Well, actually I didn't watch you much. What it comes down to is that I'm pretty apolitical, you know?"

Alessi forced another half-smile. "I could have used your vote."

"I wasn't registered."

Alessi shrugged mentally and returned his attention to the awesome drop-offs that tugged at the car on Lakey's side. Gravel and raw rock gave way to forest and then to valley floor. Much of the valley was cleared and quilted with irrigated squares. It's a much tamer country than when I left, Alessi thought.

"I'm really sorry I didn't vote."

"What?" Distracted, Alessi swerved slightly to avoid two fist-sized rocks that had rolled onto the right-hand lane probably during the night.

"I think you're a nice man. I said I'm sorry I didn't vote."

"It's a little late for that." Alessi envenomed the words. He heard the tone of pettiness, recognized it, said the words anyway.

"Don't blame me, Mr. Alessi," she said. "Really, I'm not stupid. You can't blame me for losing . . . Senator."

I'm being reproached, he thought, by a drop-out, wet-behind-the-ears girl. Me, a fifty-seven-year-old man. A fifty-seven-year-old unemployable. God damn it! The rage he thought he'd exorcised in San Francisco rose up again. He thought the rim of the steering wheel would shatter under his fingers into jagged, slashing shards.

Lakey must have seen something in his eyes. She moved back across the front seat and wedged herself uneasily into the juncture of bench seat and door. "You, uh, all right?"

"Yes," said Alessi. He willed the muscles cording his neck to relax, with little effect. "I am very sorry I snapped at you, Sally."

"It's okay." But she looked dubious of the sincerity of his apology.

They rode in silence for another few miles. She'll talk, thought Alessi. Sooner or later.

Sooner. "How soon?"

"Before we get to the house? Not long. The turnoff's another few miles." And what the hell, he asked himself, are you doing taking a kid little better than a third your age to the half-remembered refuge where you're going to whimper, crawl in and pull the hole in after you? It's perhaps the worst time in your life and you're acting the part of a horny old man. You've known her a grand total of eight hours. No, he answered himself. More than that. She reminds me— He tensed. She asked me if she could come along. Remember? She asked me.

I see the dark-blue sedan turn into the semicircular driveway and slide between the pines toward the house. Tires crunch on drifted cones and dead leaves; the crisp sound rises toward me. I stretch to watch as the auto nears the porch and passes below the angle of my sight. The engine dies. I hear a car door slam. Another one. For some reason it had not occurred to me that Frank might bring another person.

The equations of the house must be altered.

They stood silently for a while, looking up at the house. It was a large house, set in scale by the towering mountains beyond. Wind hissed in the pine needles; otherwise the only sound was the broken buzz of a logging truck down-shifting far below on the highway.

"It's lovely," Lakey said.

"That's the original building." Alessi pointed. "My father put it together in the years before the First World War. The additions were constructed over a period of decades."

"It must have twenty rooms."

"Ought to have been a hotel," said Alessi. "Never was. Dad liked baronial space. Some of the rooms are sealed off, never used."

"What's that?" Lakey stabbed a finger at the third floor. "The thing that looks like a porthole."

"Old glass, my favorite window when I was a kid. Behind it is a room that's been used variously as a nursery, playroom and guest room."

Lakey stared at the glass. "I thought I saw something move."

"Probably a tree shadow, or maybe a squirrel's gotten in. It wasn't the caretaker—I phoned ahead last night; he's in bed with his arthritis. Nobody else has been in the house in close to twenty years."

"I did see something," she said stubbornly.

"It isn't haunted."

She looked at him with a serious face. "How do you know?"

"No one ever died in there."

Lakey shivered. "I'm cold."

"We're at seven thousand feet." He took a key from an inside pocket of his coat. "Come in and I'll make a fire."

"Will you check the house first?"

"Better than that," he said, "*we* will check the house."

The buzz of voices drifts to the window. I am loath to leave my position behind the glass. Steps, one set heavier, one lighter, sound on the front walk. Time seems suspended as I wait for the sound of a key inserted into the latch. I anticipate the door opening. Not wanting to surprise the pair, I settle back.

Though they explored the old house together, Lakey kept forging ahead as though to assert her courage. Fine, thought Alessi. If there is something lurking in a closet, let it jump out and get *her*. The thought was only whimsical; he was a rational man.

Something did jump out of a closet at her—or at least it seemed to. Lakey opened the door at the far end of a second-floor bedroom and recoiled. A stack of photographs, loose and in albums displaced from precarious balance on the top shelf, cascaded to her feet. A plume of fine dust rose.

"There's always avalanche danger in the mountains," said Alessi.

She stopped coughing. "Very funny." Lakey knelt and picked up a sheaf of pictures. "Your family?"

Alessi studied the photographs over her shoulder. "Family, friends, holidays, vacation shots. Everyone in the family had a camera."

"You too?"

He took the corner of a glossy landscape between thumb and forefinger. "At one time I wanted to be a Stieglitz or a Cartier-Bresson, or even a Mathew Brady. Do you see the fuzz of smoke?"

She examined the photograph closely. "No."

"That's supposed to be a forest fire. I was not a good photographer. Photographs capture the present, and that in turn immediately becomes the past. My father insistently directed me to the future."

Lakey riffled through the pictures and stopped at one portrait. Except for his dress, the man might have doubled for Alessi. His gray hair was cut somewhat more severely than the Senator's. He sat stiffly upright behind a wooden desk, staring directly at the camera.

Alessi answered the unspoken question. "My father."

"He looks very distinguished," said Lakey. Her gaze

flickered up to meet his. "So do you."

"He wanted something more of a dynasty than what he got. But he tried to mold one; he really did. Every inch a mover and shaker," Alessi said sardonically. "He stayed here in the mountains and raped a fortune."

"Raped?" she said.

"Reaped. Raped. No difference. The timber went for progress and, at the time, nobody objected. My father taught me about power and I learned the lessons well. When he deemed me prepared, he sent me out to amass my own fortune in power—political, not oil or uranium. I went to the legislature and then to Washington. Now I'm home again."

"Home," she said, softening his word. "I think maybe you're leaving out some things." He didn't answer. She stopped at another picture. "Is this your mother?"

"No." He stared at the sharp features for several seconds. "That is Mrs. Norrinssen, an ironbound, more-Swedish-than-thou, pagan lady who came out here from someplace in the Dakotas. My father hired her to—take care of me in lieu of my mother."

Lakey registered his hesitation, then said uncertainly, "What happened to your mother?"

Alessi silently sorted through the remainder of the photographs. Toward the bottom of the stack, he found what he was looking for and extracted it. A slender woman, short-haired and of extraordinary beauty, stared past the camera; or perhaps *through* the camera. Her eyes had a distant, unfocused quality. She stood in a stand of dark spruce, her hands folded.

"It's such a moody picture," said Lakey.

The pines loomed above Alessi's mother, conical bodies appearing to converge in the upper portion of the grainy print. "I took that," said Alessi. "She didn't know. It was the last picture anyone took of her."

"She . . . died?"

"Not exactly. I suppose so. No one knows."

"I don't understand," said Lakey.

"She was a brilliant, lonely, unhappy lady," said Alessi. "My father brought her out here from Florida. She hated it. The mountains oppressed her; the winters depressed her. Every year she retreated further into herself. My father tried to bring her out of it, but he treated her like a child. She resisted his pressures. Nothing seemed to work." He lapsed again into silence.

Finally Lakey said, "What happened to her?"

"It was after Mrs. Norrinssen had been here for two years. My mother's emotional state had been steadily deteriorating. Mrs. Norrinssen was the only one who could talk with her, or perhaps the only one with whom my mother would talk. One autumn day—it was in October. My mother got up before everyone else and walked out into the woods. That was that."

"That can't be all," said Lakey. "Didn't anyone look?"

"Of course we looked. My father hired trackers and dogs and the sheriff brought in his searchers. They trailed her deep into the pine forest and then lost her. They spent weeks. Then the snows increased and they gave up. There's a stone out behind the house in a grove, but no one's buried under it."

"Jesus," Lakey said softly. She put her arms around Alessi and gave him a slow, warm hug. The rest of the photographs fluttered to the hardwood floor.

I wait. I wait. I see no necessity of movement, not for now. I am patient. No longer do I go to the round window. My vigil is being rewarded. There is no reason to watch the unknowing birds, the forest, the road. The clouds have no message for me today.

I hear footsteps on the stair, and that is message enough.

"Most of the attic," said Alessi, "was converted into a nursery for me. My father always looked forward. He believed in constant renovation. As I became older, the nursery evolved to a playroom, though it was still the room where I slept. After my father died, I moved back here with my family for a few years. This was Connie's room."

"Your wife or your—"

"Daughter. For whatever reason, she preferred this to all the other rooms."

They stood just inside the doorway. The playroom extended most of the length of the house. Alessi imagined he could see the straight, carefully crafted lines of construction curving toward one another in perspective. Three dormer windows were spaced evenly along the eastern pitch of the ceiling. The round window allowed light to enter at the far end.

"It's huge," said Lakey.

"It outscales children. It was an adventure to live here. Sometimes it was very easy for me to imagine I was playing in a jungle or on a sea, or across a trackless Arctic waste."

"Wasn't it scary?"

"My father didn't allow that," said Alessi. Nor did I later on, he thought.

Lakey marveled. "The furnishings are incredible." The canopied bed, the dressers and vanity, the shelves and chairs, all were obviously products of the finest woodcraft. "Not a piece of plastic in all this." She laughed. "I love it." In her denim jeans and Pendleton shirt, she pirouetted. She stopped in front of a set of walnut shelves. "Are these dolls your daughter's?"

Alessi nodded. "My father was not what you would call a liberated man. Connie collected them all during her childhood." He carefully picked up a figure with a silk nineteenth-century dress and china head.

Lakey eagerly moved from object to object like a butterfly sampling flowers. "That horse! I always wanted one."

"My father made it for me. It's probably the most exactingly carpentered hobbyhorse made."

Lakey gingerly seated herself on the horse. Her feet barely touched the floor. "It's so big." She rocked back and forth, leaning against the leather reins. Not a joint squeaked.

Alessi said, "He scaled it so it would be a child's horse, not a pony. You might call these training toys for small adults."

The woman let the horse rock to a stop. She dismounted and slowly approached a tubular steel construction. A six-foot horizontal ladder connected the top rungs of two vertical four-foot ladders. "What on earth is this?"

Alessi was silent for a few seconds. "That is a climbing toy for three- and four-year-olds."

"But it's too big," said Lakey. "Too high."

"Not," said Alessi, "with your toes on one rung and your fingers on the next—just barely."

"It's impossible."

Alessi shook his head. "Not quite; just terrifying."

"But why?" she said. "Did you do this for fun?"

"Dad told me to. When I balked, he struck me. When he had to, my father never discounted the effect of force."

Lakey looked disconcerted. She turned away from the skeletal bridge toward a low table shoved back against the wall.

"Once there was a huge map of fairyland on the wall above the table," said Alessi. "Mrs. Norrinssen gave it to me. I can remember the illustrations, the ogres and frost giants and fairy castles. In a rage one night, my father ripped it to pieces."

Lakey knelt before the table so she could look on a level with the stuffed animals. "It's a whole zoo!" She reached out to touch the plush hides.

"More than a zoo," said Alessi. "A complete bestiary. Some of these critters don't exist. See the unicorn on the end?"

Lakey's attention was elsewhere. "The bear," she said, greedily reaching like a small child. "He's beautiful. I had one like him when I was little." She gathered the stuffed bear into her arms and hugged it. The creature was almost half her size. "What's his name? I called mine Bear. Is he yours?"

Alessi nodded. "And my daughter's. His name is Bear too. Mrs. Norrinssen made him."

She traced her finger along the bear's head, over his ears, down across the snout. Bear's hide was virtually seamless, sewn out of some rich pile fabric. After all the years, Bear's eyes were still black and shiny.

"The eyes came from the same glazier who cut the round window. Good nineteenth-century glass."

"This is wild," said Lakey. She touched the teeth.

"I don't really know whether it was Mrs. Norrinssen's idea or my father's," said Alessi. "A hunter supplied them. They're real. Mrs. Norrinssen drilled small holes toward the back of each tooth; they're secured inside the lining." Bear's mouth was lined with black leather, pliable to Lakey's questing finger. "Don't let him bite you."

"Most bears' mouths are closed," said Lakey.

"Yes."

"It didn't stop my Bear from talking to me."

"Mine didn't have to overcome that barrier." Alessi suddenly listened to what he was saying. Fifty-seven years old. He smiled self-consciously.

They stood silently for a few seconds; Lakey continued to hug the bear. "It's getting dark," she said. The sun had set while they explored the house. The outlines of solid shapes in the playroom had begun to blur with twilight. Doll faces shone almost luminously in the dusk.

"We'll get the luggage out of the car," said Alessi.

"Could I stay up here?"

"You mean tonight?" She nodded. "I see no reason why not," he said. He thought, did I really plan this?

Lakey stepped closer. "What about you?"

I watch them both. Frank Alessi very much resembles his father: distinguished. He looks harried, worn, but that is understandable. Some information I comprehend without knowing why. Some perceptions I don't have to puzzle over. I know what I see.

The woman is in her early twenties. She has mobile features, a smiling, open face. She is quick to react. Her eyes are as dark as her black hair. They dart back and forth in their sockets, her gaze lighting upon nearly everything in the room but rarely dwelling. Her speech is rapid with a hint of eastern nasality. Except for her manner of speaking, she reminds me of a dear memory.

For a moment I see four people standing in the playroom. Two are reflections in the broad, hand-silvered mirror above the vanity across the room. Two people are real. They hesitantly approach each other, a step at a time. Their arms extend, hands touch, fingers plait. Certainly at this time, in this place, they have found each other. The mirror images are inexact, but I think only I see that. The couple in the mirror seem to belong to another time. And, of course, I am there in the mirror too—though no one notices me.

"That's, uh, very gratifying to my ego," said Alessi. "But do you know how old I am?"

Lakey nodded. The semidarkness deepened. "I have some idea."

"I'm old enough to—"

"—be my father. I know." She said lightly, "So?"

"So . . ." He took his hands from hers. In the early night

dolls seemed to watch them. The shiny button eyes of Bear and the other animals appeared turned toward the human pair.

"Yes," she said. "I think it's a good idea." She took his hand again. "Come on, we'll get the stuff out of the car. It's been a long day."

Day, Alessi thought. Long week, long month, longer campaign. A lifetime. The headlines flashed in his mind, television commentaries replayed. It all stung like acid corroding what had been cold, shining and clean. Old, old, old, like soldiers and gunfighters. How had he missed being cleanly shot? Enough had seemed to want that. To fade . . .

"I *am* a little bushed," he said. He followed Lakey out toward the stairs.

Frank Alessi's father was forceful in his ideal. That lent the foundation to that time and this place. Strength was virtue. "Fair is fair," he would say, but the fairness was all his. Such power takes time to dissipate. Mrs. Norrinssen stood up to that force; everyone else eventually fled.

"Witchy bitch!" he would storm. She only stared back at him from calm, glacial eyes until he sputtered and snorted and came to rest like a great, sulky, but now gentled beast. Mrs. Norrinssen was a woman of extraordinary powers and she tapped ancient reserves.

Structure persists. I am part of it. That is my purpose and I cannot turn aside. Now I wait in the newly inhabited house. Again I hear the positive, metallic sounds of automobile doors and a trunk lid opening and closing. I hear the voices and the footsteps and appreciate the human touch they lend.

She stretched slowly. "What time is it?"
"Almost ten," said Alessi.
"I saw you check your watch. I thought you'd be asleep.

Not enough exercise?"

She giggled and Alessi was surprised to find the sound did not offend him as it had earlier in the day. He rolled back toward her and lightly kissed her lips. "Plenty of exercise."

"You were really nice."

Fingertips touched his face, exploring cheekbones, mouth corners, the stubble on the jowl line. That made him slightly nervous; his body was still tight. Tennis, handball, swimming, it all helped. Reasonably tight. Only slight concessions to slackness. But after all, he *was*— Shut up, he told himself.

"I feel very comfortable with you," she said.

Don't talk, he thought. Don't spoil it.

Lakey pressed close. "Say something."

No.

"Are you nervous?"

"No," Alessi said. "Of course not."

"I guess I did read about the divorce," said Lakey. "It was in a picture magazine in my gynecologist's office."

"There isn't much to say. Marge couldn't take the heat. She got out. I can't blame her." But silently he denied that. The Watergate people—*their* wives stood by. All the accumulated years . . . Betrayal is so goddamned nasty. Wish her well in Santa Fe?

"Tell me about your daughter," said Lakey.

"Connie—why her?"

"You've talked about everyone else. You haven't said a thing about Connie except to say she slept in this room." She paused. "In this bed?"

"We both did," said Alessi, "at different times."

"The stuff about the divorce didn't really mention her, at least not that I remember. Where is she?"

"I truly don't know."

Lakey's voice sounded peculiar. "She disappeared, uh, just like—"

"No. She left." Silently: she left me. Just like—

"You haven't heard from her? Nothing?"

"Not in several years. It was her choice; we didn't set detectives on her. The last we heard, she was living in the street in some backwater college town in Colorado."

"I mean, you didn't try—"

"It was her choice." She always said I didn't *allow* her any choice, he thought. Maybe. But I tried to handle her as my father handled me. And *I* turned out—

"What was she like?"

Alessi caressed her long smooth hair; static electricity snapped and flashed. "Independent, intelligent, lovely. I suppose fathers tend to be biased."

"How old is she?"

"Connie was about your age when she left." He realized he had answered the question in the past tense.

"You're not so old yourself," said Lakey, touching him strategically. "Not old at all."

Moonlight floods through the dormer panes; beyond the round window I see starlight fleck the sky. I am very quiet, though I need not be. The couple under the quilted coverlet are enthralled in their passion. I cannot question their motives yet. Love? I doubt it. Affection? I would approve of that. Physical attraction, craving for bodily contact, psychic tension?

I move to my window in the end of the playroom, leaving the love-making behind. The aesthetics of the bed are not as pleasing as the placid starfield. It may be that I am accustomed to somewhat more stately cycles and pulsings.

Perhaps it is the crowding of the house, the apprehension that more than one human body dwells within it, that causes me now to feel a loneliness. I wonder where Mrs. Norrinssen settled after the untimely death of her employer. "A bad bargain," he said somberly time after time. "Very bad indeed." And she only smiled back, never maliciously or with humor, but patiently. She had given him what he wanted. "But still a bargain," she said.

I am aware of the sounds subsiding from the canopied bed. I wonder if both now will abandon themselves to dreams and to sleep. A shadow dips silently past the window, a nighthawk. Faintly I hear the cries of hunting birds.

He came awake suddenly with teeth worrying his guilty soul. Connie glared at him from dark eyes swollen from crying and fury. She shook long black hair back from her shoulders. ". . . drove her through the one breakdown and into another." He dimly heard the words. "She's out of it, and good for her. No more campaigns. You won't do the same to me, you son of a bitch." Bitter smile. "Or I should say, you son of a bastard."

"I can't change these things. I'm just trying—" Alessi realized he was shaking in the darkness.

"What's wrong, now what's wrong?" said Connie.

Alessi cried out once, low.

"Baby, what is it?"

He saw Lakey's face in the pooled moonlight. "You." He reached out to touch her cheek and grazed her nose.

"Me," she said. "Who else?"

"Jesus," Alessi said. "Oh God."

"Bad dream?"

Orientation slowly settled in. "A nightmare." He shook his head violently.

"Tell me about it."

"I can't remember."

"So don't tell me if you don't want to." She gathered him close, blotting the sweat on his sternum with the sheet.

He said dreamily, "You always plan to make it up, but

after a while it's too late."

"What's too late?"

Alessi didn't answer. He lay rigid beside her.

I see them in the gilt-framed mirror and I see them in bed. I feel both a terrible sympathy for her and a terrible love for him. For as long as I can recall, I've husbanded proprietary feelings about this house and those in it.

Frank Alessi makes me understand. I remember the woman's touch and cherish that feeling, though I simultaneously realize her touch was yet another's. I also remember Frank's embrace. I have touched all of them.

I love all these people. That terrifies me.

I want to tell him, you *can* change things, Frank.

Sometime after midnight he awoke again. The night had encroached; moonlight now filled less than a quarter of the playroom. Alessi lay still, staring at shadow patterns. He heard Lakey's soft, regular breathing beside him.

He lay without moving for what seemed to be hours. When he checked his watch only minutes had passed. Recumbent, he waited, assuming that for which he waited was sleep.

Sleep had started to settle about Alessi when he thought he detected a movement across the room. Part vague movement, part snatch of sound, it was *something.* Switching on the bedtable lamp, Alessi saw nothing. He held his breath for long seconds and listened. Still nothing. The room held only its usual complement of inhabitants: dolls, toys, stuffed creatures. Bear stared back at him. The furniture was all familiar. Everything was in its place, natural. He felt his pulse speeding. He turned off the light and settled back against the pillow.

It's one o'clock in the soul, he thought. Not quite Fitzgerald, but it will do. He remembered Lakey in the car that afternoon asking why he had cut and run. That wasn't the exact phraseology, but it was close enough. So what if he had been forced out of office? He still could have found some kind of political employment. Alessi had not told her about all the records unsubpoenaed as well as subpoenaed—at first. Then, perversely, he had started to catalog the sordid details the investigating committees had decided not to use. After a while she had turned her head back toward the clean mountain scenery. He continued the list. Finally she had told him to shut up. She turned back toward him gravely, had told him it was all right—she had forgiven him. It had been simple and sincere.

I don't need easy forgiveness, he thought. Nor would *I* forgive. That afternoon he had lashed out at her. "Damn it, what do you know about these things—about responsibility and power? You're a hippie—or whatever hippies are called now. Did you ever make a single solitary decision that put you on the line? Made you a target for second-guessing, carping analysis, sniping, unabashed viciousness?" The overtaut spring wound down.

Lakey visibly winced; muscles tightened around her mouth. "Yes," she said.

"So tell me."

She stared back at him like a small surprised animal. "I've been traveling a long time. Before I left, I was pregnant." Her voice flattened; Alessi strained to hear the words. "They told me it should have been a daughter."

He focused his attention back on the road. There was nothing to say. He knew about exigencies. He could approve.

"None of them wanted me to do it. They made it more than it really was. When I left, my parents told me they would never speak to me again. They haven't."

Alessi frowned.

"I loved them."

Alessi heard her mumble, make tiny incoherent sounds. She shifted in her sleep in a series of irregular movements. Her voice raised slightly in volume. The words still were unintelligible. Alessi recognized the tenor; she was dreaming of fearful things. He stared intently; his vision blurred.

Gently he gathered Connie into his arms and stroked her hair. "I will make it right for you. I know, I know . . . I can."

"No," she said, the word sliding into a moan. Sharply, "No."

"I am your father."

But she ignored him.

I hear more than I can see. I hear the woman come fully awake, her moans sliding raggedly up the register to screams; pain—not love; shock—not passion. I would rather not listen, but I have no choice. So I hear the desperation of a body whose limbs are trapped between strangling linens and savage lover. I hear the endless, pounding slap of flesh against meat. Finally I hear the words, the words, the cruel words and the ineffectual. Worst of all, I hear the cries. I hear them in sadness.

Earlier I could not object. But now he couples with her not out of love, not from affection, but to force her. No desire, no lust, no desperate pleasure save inarticulate power.

Finally she somehow frees herself and scrambles off the bed. She stumbles through the unfamiliar room and slams against the wall beside the door. Only her head intrudes into the moonlight, her mouth is set in a rigid, silent oval. The wet blackness around her eyes is more than shadow. She says nothing. She fumbles for the door, claws the knob, is gone. He does not pursue her.

I hear the sound of the woman's stumbling steps. I hear her pound on the doors of the car Alessi habitually locks.

The sounds of her flight diminish in the night. She will be safer with the beasts of the mountain.

Alessi endlessly slammed his fist into the bloody pillow. His body shook until the inarticulate rage began to burn away. Then he got up from the bed and crossed the playroom to the great baroque mirror.

"This time could have been different," he said. "I wanted it to be."

His eyes adjusted to the darkness. A thin sliver of moonlight striped the ceiling. Alessi confronted the creature in the mirror. He raised his hands in fists and battered them against unyielding glass, smashed them against the mirror until the surface fragmented into glittering shards. He presented his wrists, repeating in endless rote, "Different, this time, different..."

Then he sensed what lay behind him in the dark. Alessi swung around, blood arcing. Time overcame him. The warm, coppery smell rose up in the room.

Perhaps the house now is haunted; that I cannot say. My own role is ended. Again I am alone; and now lonely. This morning I have not looked through the round window. The carrion crows are inside my mind picking at the bones of memories.

I watch Frank Alessi across the stained floor of the playroom.

The house is quiet; I'm sure that will not continue. The woman will have reached the highway and surely has been found by now. She will tell her story and then the people will come.

For a time the house will be inhabited by many voices and many bodies. The people will look at Frank Alessi and his wrists and his blood. They will remark upon the shattered mirror. They may even note the toys, note me; wonder at the degree of the past preserved here in the house. I doubt they can detect the pain in my old-fashioned eyes.

They will search for answers.

But they can only question why Frank came here, and why he did what he did. They cannot see the marks left by the teeth of the past. Only the blood.

AS NEVER BEFORE, the west is a melting pot of diverse cultures and interest groups: ranchers, Native Americans, tourists, energy corporations, farmers, environmental advocates, the people who used to be called hippies, small-town dwellers, lovers of the outdoors, would-be mountain men, artists . . . It's a complex equation to which an additional element can always be added.

"Beyond the Sand River Range" first appeared in a book clearly labeled and packaged as science fiction. Yet the story doesn't seem to be anything more futuristic than a topical piece describing some contemporary people with contemporary problems in a contemporary Wyoming—until the final page. This is the oldest story in the book and reflects an earlier stage in my development as a writer. Aside from that, I won't apologize for my lack of subtlety. I include the story because I think it says something worth saying.

Beyond the Sand River Range

CALVIN KNIFEHUNTER RODE DOWN OUT OF THE SAND RIVER Range with his back to the north wind and his face to the cold stars. Wind rushed powerfully through the stands of blue spruce as the horse picked a trail down the slope. The wind shouted and Cal listened to it, ignoring the cold.

A rock dislodged under the horse's hoof and the animal's hindquarters slipped downhill as it struggled to keep equilibrium. The horse found its balance.

"Easy, girl." Below, the rattle of sliding stones diminished in the darkness. The rider nudged the mare's ribs with his heel. "Come on."

The moon began to rise as the land became level. The bleakness of the open range was softened by moonlight. The timber thinned and disappeared, but the wind remained strong as Cal rode through the low sagebrush.

There was a fence of barbed wire and a tightly stretched gate, then the last pasture before home. The mare knew she was going home and broke into a gallop. Cal rode bareback and he felt the rhythm of the horse's muscles.

Across a dry creek bed and then the dark outbuilding, Cal swung down off the mare. The horse whickered, breathing heavily, and there was foam in her jaws.

"You've had a good vacation, right, girl? You aren't used to this." Cal led the mare into the small barn. He gave her a cursory rubdown and part of a pail of oats. Then he walked to the house.

The collie Brownie, tail wagging, waited for him on the porch. Cal knelt and rubbed between the dog's ears. The man looked up at the empty rocking chair in back of Brownie. He remembered his father endlessly rocking in that chair, growing older until he died of old age at forty-six. The rocker remained, but the empty bottles had long since been thrown away.

The door opened into light and warmth. Preceded by Brownie, Cal walked into the three-room house. His mother sat reading at the table beneath the unshaded hundred-watt bulb.

Leah Marshall Knifehunter was a tired woman. She had never been pretty, but many who knew her as a girl had attributed to her what they called "spunk." She had been the daughter of a town banker in Fremont and was theoretically fated to marry high up in the aristocracy of the rural west. But chance and unexplainable impulse had intervened and Leah married Thomas Eagle Feather Knifehunter, full-blooded Shoshoni. That she "married Indian" was unforgivable. She was written out of her father's will. She was ostracized by her white friends. She was only grudgingly accepted by the Indians of the reservation. Leah had married for love.

"Was it like you remember?"

Cal sat down opposite his mother. "Yes. Four years doesn't change much up there." He was suddenly aware of the numbness in his fingers. He rubbed his hands together to warm them. "Babe's fat and lazy now. Needs to be ridden. I'll work it off her."

"You hungry?"

Cal considered. "No."

"Some venison steaks. Deer your Uncle Paul shot last winter."

"No thanks. Just not hungry. I'm going into Fremont for a while."

"Why?" There was a strange note in Leah's voice.

"Thought I'd look up some old friends."

"Be careful."

Cal laughed. "Mom, I'm not going to get in trouble. I'm a college graduate now, remember?"

His mother, grimly, "Aren't many of your old friends left."

"I know." The laughter left his voice. "But some of them aren't dead or in jail."

"Be home early?"

"Probably." His words were light again. "Mom, I'm not your baby any more."

"I know." She hesitated. "But be careful anyway."

"I will," he said, standing and taking the car keys from the table. "Keep Brownie inside until I'm gone." The last thing he saw as he closed the door was the row of old books on the shelf across the room. Worn spines and faded gilt titles: Rousseau and Bunyan, *The Book of Martyrs* and Thoreau.

The '55 Chevy bounced noisily along the two miles of ruts that joined the state highway. Cal thought of his mother making her weekly shopping trips to Fremont in this car.

Twenty miles he drove along Sand River Canyon. There was very little traffic, so he pushed the protesting engine until the car vibrated along at seventy. Then the highway angled around the flank of a mountain and Cal saw the lights of Fremont ahead. Fremont, county seat of Shoshoni County. Commercial center for the ranching community, for the reservation, for the uranium and oil people. Five thousand nice white Anglo souls, Cal thought, and wished he could work the medicine which would bring the Sand River Range sliding down on Fremont.

He was vaguely surprised at his gut reaction. Hatred, Cal thought. Maybe school didn't civilize me as much as it was intended.

The lights of Fremont grew brighter and more distinct. The road ran down a slight grade, then across the seldom-used railroad tracks and into Main Street. Downtown Fremont was five blocks of light and noise; stores, filling stations and bars. At ten o'clock on this October night, the stores were closed. But it was the third Saturday in the month. The men from the oil fields had their pay. So did the hands off the local ranches. And the Indians had their government checks.

Cal parked a block off Main and locked the car. He walked through the downtown, seeing many faces, but none familiar. Cal was suddenly thirsty and decided to get a beer.

"Hey, you! Injun! You with the funny hair!" The shout was from behind him. Cal took his hand away from the door to the Antelope Lounge and slowly turned. His fingers curled into fists. Then he involuntarily stared and pulled a double-take. "Davy! I'll be damned."

"Hey man, you look good." Davy White Hawk walked forward, grinning and holding out his hand.

"Long time," Cal said.

"Yeah. You home for good?"

"A while, maybe. Probably a year. I'm in VISTA now—be working out on the reservation. Then I figure the government'll send me to law school."

"Hey, you'll be the biggest success the tribe ever had."

"Maybe."

"You will; no sweat. How about a beer to celebrate?"

"That's what I was after when you yelled."

"At the Antelope? Hell, let's go down to the Wagon Box. They got the wildest go-go dancer you ever saw."

"I don't know," said Cal. He hesitated. "I remember before I left, the Wagon Box was kind of a hassle."

"Yeah." Davy was expressionless. "Things are different now. A little. They'll let anybody in, if they have money."

The bar was crowded and noisy. The hostess, fifty and wrinkled in red velvet, showed them to a small table close to the juke box.

"I don't think I missed much!" Cal shouted, competing with eighty decibels of Buck Owens.

"Must be the girl's taking a break," said Davy. The barmaid set a pitcher and two glasses down hard on the table, slopping beer on the Coors napkins.

"Davy, what are you doing these days?"

"Not much." He poured carefully, not allowing a head to foam on the beer. "This and that. You know."

"Yeah, I know."

Someone lurched against the table and a wave of alcoholic breath made Cal think of a rotting carcass under the sun. By his stained work clothes a wildcatter down from the drilling rigs in the hills, the man surveyed Cal and Davy with bleary eyes. "Hey, boys," he said, slurring the 's.' "What time you dance?"

Davy half-rose, pulling back his right fist. Cal stood and grabbed his arm. "No," Cal said. "Come on."

Outside, Cal said, "Maybe things haven't changed."

"Maybe not." Davy's jaw was set tense; the skin stretched tight over high cheekbones. "We should have killed that son of a bitch."

And it all flowed back through Cal's memory, as if borne by the wind which lashed around the mercury street lamps.

Four years before. The rain had fallen in sporadic showers of large, chill drops, settling finally to a steady drizzle. The gray thunderheads had rolled, been torn apart by the wind and reunited high over the Sand Rivers. And at two in the morning, Davy's little sister Mickey had stumbled through the puddles to the Knifehunter house.

Davy needed help, she had said. They were looking for Richard, their older brother. He had gone to Fremont in the afternoon for groceries. He hadn't come back. Awakened at midnight, a sleepy grocer claimed indignantly on the phone that he hadn't seen Richard White Hawk at all. So Davy started the search.

It was Cal, Davy and Lattimer, the Indian Agent, who found him finally. As they rounded a rainslick curve by the canyon, the brights picked up a reflected gleam that could have been the eyes of an animal. They braked and looked closer and saw the skid marks black under the sheet of rain. They parked Lattimer's big Oldsmobile on the shoulder of the state highway and let the lights play on the shining object. Ungracefully the three slid down the slick grass of the embankment.

"Over here!"

The object was a chrome hubcap from a Ford pickup. The three probed beyond and turned on their flashlights. They found the truck itself about forty yards further. It lay upside down, masked from the road by clumps of tall willows.

Sick at what he knew he would find, Cal pushed ahead of Davy and shone his light in the cab. Richard was still there. Sprawled half out of the window of the cab, he had been pinned by the crushed roof. He lay face down. The coroner said at the inquest that Richard White Hawk had drowned in an inch of muddy water. The ruling had been accidental death as a result of driving while intoxicated (there was a half-empty fifth of cheap whiskey under the seat).

But before that, on the stormy mountainside, Davy had found a deeper reason for his brother's death. He had knelt and lifted his brother's head out of the puddled rain and cradled it silently for a few minutes. Then he had looked up at Lattimer, his face as rigid as the Sand River granite.

"You did this," he said to the Indian Agent. And that was all.

Four years later, Cal remembered the white man's eyes, pitying and paternal, as they looked silently away.

You did this, Cal's mind had echoed. Three words too simple, but sufficient. And he knew then he would do anything, even go to the white man's college, to keep it from happening again.

"Hello, Cal."

Cal looked back and saw the same eyes, four years older, surrounded by more wrinkles, but the same blue eyes. "Hello," he said.

Donald Lattimer was a career man in the Bureau of Indian Affairs. He was a kind man, and a conscientious man, and he did for "his people" what he thought was right. But he was white and there were many things about his job which he could never know.

The Indian Agent walked up to them, smiling, "Hello, Davy."

"Excuse me, I got to see somebody. See you, Cal." He turned and hurried down the sidewalk.

"We sure are proud of you, son," Lattimer said, pumping Cal's hand enthusiastically. "And coming back to help your people—well, all we can say is, that's great."

"Yeah." Come off it, thought Cal.

The white man looked weary. "You still dislike me, don't you, Cal?"

"Yes."

"Why?"

Cal didn't answer.

Lattimer said, "Son, you're too much a romantic. You're really caught up emotionally in your people's whole tradition and history. Don't fight the war that ended long ago."

"I am?"

"It's over. We're not the same people who drove you out of your forests and plains and broke the treaties."

Cal was suddenly, unaccountably angry. "No? How many names should I call out? Wounded Knee, 1890. Three hundred Sioux civilians, men, women and children, massacred by U.S. troopers. Times have changed? Check your newspapers, man."

Lattimer's expression was patient. "When you were on that scholarship in California, did you take an anthropology course?"

"Yes."

"And do you remember learning anything about two cultures on a collision course?"

Cal realized he might have underestimated the man. He said, as though quoting the textbook, "In the conflict of two societies, the technologically superior culture usually emerges dominant."

"Not *usually*, Cal. *Always*. History bears that out."

"*No!*"

Lattimer looked down at the dirty, cracked pavement. "Part of the losing culture may survive; often it may subvert a part of the victor. But its culture, as an entire pattern, is smashed." He raised his head and looked Cal in the eye. "That happens and both sides have to accept it. They have to work with it."

Cal's words were very low and clear. "Man, you're arrogant. So goddamned arrogant. And someday it's going to bring you down."

"I'm sorry. I'm just trying to be honest."

Something was wrong. Cal looked around and realized he and Lattimer were alone on the street. There was a metallic rattle as the wind drove an empty aluminum beer can down the sidewalk. It rolled against Cal's boot and stopped.

Down the block the door of the Antelope Lounge opened and Davy White Hawk ran down the street toward them.

"Where is everybody?" Cal yelled.

"Inside. Watching TV in the bars. Man, you're missing it. Biggest show of the century." Davy was gasping, out of breath.

"What's this?" said Lattimer.

"News show, every channel. Goddamn aliens."

"Aliens?" Lattimer looked puzzled.

"Space people, somebody. Flying saucer or something. Big round thing, glows white, big as a goddamn mountain. Landed outside New York."

For once Lattimer's fatherly composure was disturbed. "This is true?"

Davy stared. "So help me, it's true. Big goddamn round thing. TV says it's from another star or something. Scientists figure they're maybe thousands of years ahead of us."

The wind rose and whistled around the cornices of the Shoshoni County Courthouse on the next block.

"A thousand years ahead," said Cal.

Lattimer was not an unintelligent man. He turned away as Cal looked up at the cold stars above the Sand River Range and began to laugh.

"STRATA" IS THE longest and most complex piece of writing about Wyoming I've done so far. In many respects it's a love letter to the state in which I spent twenty-odd years; in others, it's a kind of signpost to the novel about Wyoming I will eventually do. There will likely be more than one book from me about the west. They will come after I conquer my irrational fear of writing pieces of fiction longer than about 15,000 words. In the meantime, I'll continue my love affair with the short fiction mode.

I truly had a ball doing what I might term a scientific ghost story about the Wind River Canyon. People ask where writers get their ideas. The valid answer, of course, is "everywhere." Stories generate from vivid images seen from a car driving on I-80 across the Red Desert, from a stranded ranch hand encountered at the bus station at the LaRamie Hotel in Wheatland, from a conversational scrap overheard at a branding west of Sundance, or from a hundred thousand other incidents. The writer has to keep eyes and ears and all the other senses open and receptive. "Strata" germinated from a single image: the road signs placed in Wind River Canyon by the Highway Department to let motorists know through which geological epoch they are traveling as the highway cuts through the living rock. I can think of no more eloquent argument for time travel.

Strata

Six hundred million years in thirty-two miles. Six hundred million years in fifty-one minutes. Steve Mavrakis traveled in time—courtesy of the Wyoming Highway Department. The epochs raveled between Thermopolis and Shoshoni. The Wind River rambled down its canyon with the Burlington Northern tracks cut into the west walls, and the two-lane blacktop, U.S. 20, sliced into the east. Official signs driven into the verge of the highway proclaimed the traveler's progress:

DINWOODY FORMATION
TRIASSIC
185-225 MILLION YEARS

BIG HORN FORMATION
ORDOVICIAN
440-500 MILLION YEARS

FLATHEAD FORMATION
CAMBRIAN
500-600 MILLION YEARS

The mileposts might have been staked into the canyon rock under the pressure of millennia. They were there for those who could not read the stone.

Tonight Steve ignored the signs. He had made this run many times before. Darkness hemmed him. November clawed when he cracked the window to exhaust Camel smoke from the Chevy's cab. The CB crackled occasionally and picked up exactly nothing.

The wind blew—that was nothing unusual. Steve felt himself hypnotized by the skiff of snow skating across the pavement in the glare of his brights. The snow swirled only inches above the blacktop, rushing across like surf sliding over the black packed sand of a beach.

Time's predator hunts.

Years scatter before her like a school of minnows surprised. The rush of her passage causes eons to eddy. Wind sweeps down the canyon with the roar of combers breaking on the sand. The moon, full and newly risen, exerts its tidal force.

Moonlight flashes on the slash of teeth.

And Steve snapped alert, realized he had traversed the thirty-two miles, crossed the flats leading into Shoshoni, and was approaching the junction with U.S. 26. Road hypnosis? he thought. Safe in Shoshoni, but it was scary. He didn't remember a goddamned minute of the trip through the canyon! Steve rubbed his eyes with his left hand and looked for an open cafe with coffee.

It hadn't been the first time.

All those years before, the four of them had thought they were beating the odds. On a chill night in June, high on a mountain edge in the Wind River Range, high on more than mountain air, the four of them celebrated graduation. They were young and clear-eyed: ready for the world. That night they knew there were no other people for miles. Having learned in class that there were 3.8 human beings per square mile in Wyoming, and as *four,* they thought the odds outnumbered.

Paul Onoda, eighteen. He was Sansei—third-generation Japanese-American. In 1942, before he was conceived, his parents were removed with eleven thousand other Japanese-Americans from California to the Heart Mountain Relocation Center in northern Wyoming. Twelve members and three generations of the Onodas shared one of four hundred and sixty-five crowded, tar-papered barracks for the next four years. Two died. Three more were born. With their fellows, the Onodas helped farm eighteen hundred acres of virgin agricultural land. Not all of them had been Japanese gardeners or truck farmers in California, so the pharmacists and the teachers and the carpenters learned agriculture. They used irrigation to bring in water. The crops flourished. The Nisei not directly involved with farming were dispatched from camp to be seasonal farm laborers. An historian later laconically noted that "Wyoming benefited by their presence."

Paul remembered the Heart Mountain camps only through the memories of his elders, but those recollections were vivid. After the war, most of the Onodas stayed on in Wyoming. With some difficulty, they bought farms. The family invested thrice the effort of their neighbors, and prospered.

Paul Onoda excelled in the classrooms and starred on the football field of Fremont High School. Once he overheard the president of the school board tell the coach, "By God but that little Nip can run!" He thought about that; and kept on running ever faster.

More than a few of his classmates secretly thought he had it all. When prom time came in his senior year, it did not go unnoticed that Paul had an extraordinarily handsome appearance to go with his brains and athlete's body. In and around Fremont, a great many concerned parents admonished their white daughters to find a good excuse if Paul asked them to the prom.

Carroll Dale, eighteen. It became second nature early on to explain to people first hearing her given name that it had two r's and two l's. Both sides of her family went back four generations in this part of the country and one of her bequests had been a proud mother. Cordelia Carroll had pride, one daughter, and the desire to see the Hereford Carrolls retain *some* parity with the Angus Dales. After all, the Carrolls had been ranching on Bad Water Creek before John Broderick Okie illuminated his Lost Cabin castle with carbide lights. That was when Teddy Roosevelt had been president and it was when all the rest of the cattlemen in Wyoming, including the Dales, had been doing their accounts at night by kerosene lanterns.

Carroll grew up to be a good roper and a better rider. Her apprenticeship intensified after her older brother, her only brother, fatally shot himself during deer season. She wounded her parents when she neither married a man who would take over the ranch nor decided to take over the ranch herself.

She grew up slim and tall, with ebony hair and large, dark, slightly oblique eyes. Her father's father, at family Christmas dinners, would overdo the whiskey in the eggnog and make jokes about Indians in the woodpile until her paternal grandmother would tell him to shut the hell up before she gave him a goodnight the hard way, with a rusty sickle and knitting needles. It was years before Carroll knew what her grandmother meant.

In junior high, Carroll was positive she was eight feet tall in Lilliput. The jokes hurt. But her mother told her to be patient, that the other girls would catch up. Most of the girls didn't; but in high school the boys did, though they tended to be tongue-tied in the extreme when they talked to her.

She was the first girl president of her school's National Honor Society. She was a cheerleader. She was the valedictorian of her class and earnestly quoted John F. Kennedy in her graduation address. Within weeks of graduation, she eloped with the captain of the football team.

It nearly caused a lynching.

Steve Mavrakis, eighteen. Courtesy allowed him to be called a native despite his birth eighteen hundred miles to the east. His parents, on the other hand, had settled in the state after the war when he was less than a year old. Given another decade, the younger native-born might grudgingly concede their adopted roots; the old-timers, never.

Steve's parents had read Zane Grey and *The Virginian,* and had spent many summers on dude ranches in upstate New York. So they found a perfect ranch on the Big Horn River and started a herd of registered Hereford. They went broke. They refinanced and aimed at a breed of inferior beef cattle. The snows of '49 killed those. Steve's father determined that sheep were the way to go—all those double and triple births. Very investment-effective. The sheep sickened, or stumbled and fell into creeks where they drowned, or panicked like turkeys and smothered in heaps in fenced corners. It occurred then to the Mavrakis family that wheat doesn't stampede. All the fields were promptly hailed out before what looked to be a bounty harvest. Steve's father gave up and moved into town where he put his Columbia degree to work by getting a job managing the district office for the Bureau of Land Management.

All of that taught Steve to be wary of sure things.

And occasionally he wondered at the dreams. He had been very young when the blizzards killed the cattle. But though he didn't remember the National Guard dropping hay bales from silver C-47's to cattle in twelve-foot-deep snow, he did recall for years after, the nightmares of herds of nonplused animals futilely grazing barren ground before towering, slowly grinding bluffs of ice.

The night after the crop-duster terrified the sheep and seventeen had expired in paroxysms, Steve dreamed of brown men shrilling and shaking sticks and stampeding tusked, hairy monsters off a precipice and down hundreds of feet to a shallow stream.

Summer nights Steve woke sweating, having dreamed of reptiles slithering and warm waves beating on a ragged beach in the lower pasture. He sat straight, staring out the bedroom window, watching the giant ferns waver and solidify back into cottonwood and boxelder.

The dreams came less frequently and vividly as he grew older. He willed that. They altered when the family moved into Fremont. After a while Steve still remembered he had had the dreams, but most of the details were forgotten.

At first the teachers in Fremont High School thought he was stupid. Steve was administered tests and thereafter was labeled an underachiever. He did what he had to do to get by. He barely qualified for the college-bound program, but then his normally easy-going father made threats. People asked him what he wanted to do, to be, and he answered honestly that he didn't know. Then he took a speech class. Drama fascinated him and he developed a passion for what theater the school offered. He played well in *Our Town* and *Arsenic and Old Lace* and *Harvey*. The drama coach looked at Steve's average height and average looks and average brown hair and eyes, and suggested at a hilarious cast party that he become either a character actor or an FBI agent.

By this time, the only dreams Steve remembered were sexual fantasies about girls he didn't dare ask on dates.

Ginger McClelland, seventeen. Who could blame her for feeling out of place? Having been born on the cusp of the school district's regulations, she was very nearly a year younger than her classmates. She was short. She thought of herself as a dwarf in a world of Snow Whites. It didn't help that her mother studiously offered words like "petite" and submitted that the most gorgeous clothes would fit a wearer under five feet, two inches. Secretly she hoped that in one mysterious night she would bloom and grow great, long legs like Carroll Dale. That never happened.

Being an exile in an alien land didn't help either. Though Carroll had befriended her, she had listened to the president of the pep club, the queen of Job's Daughters, and half the girls in her math class refer to her as "the foreign exchange student." Except that she would never be repatriated home; at least not until she graduated. Her parents had tired of living in Cupertino, California, and thought that running a Coast to Coast hardware franchise in Fremont would be an adventurous change of pace. They loved the open spaces, the mountains and free-flowing streams. Ginger wasn't so sure. Every day felt like she had stepped into a time machine. All the music on the radio was old. The movies that turned up at the town's one theater—forget it. The dancing at the hops was grotesque.

Ginger McClelland was the first person in Fremont—and perhaps in all of Wyoming—to use the adjective "bitchin'." It got her sent home from study hall and caused a bemused and confusing interview between her parents and the principal.

Ginger learned not to trust most of the boys who invited her out on dates. They all seemed to feel some sort of perverse mystique about California girls. But she did accept Steve Mavrakis's last-minute invitation to prom. He seemed safe enough.

Because Carroll and Ginger were friends, the four of them ended up double-dating in Paul's father's old maroon DeSoto that was customarily used for hauling fence posts and wire out to the pastures. After the dance, when nearly everyone else was heading to one of the sanctioned after-prom parties, Steve affably obtained from an older intermediary an entire case of chilled Hamms. Ginger and Carroll had brought along jeans and Pendleton shirts in their overnight bags and changed in the restroom at the Chevron station. Paul and Steve took off their white jackets and donned windbreakers. Then they all drove up into the Wind River Range. After they ran out of road, they hiked. It was very late and very dark. But they found a high mountain place where they huddled and drank beer and talked and necked.

They heard the voice of the wind and nothing else beyond that. They saw no lights of cars or outlying cabins. The isolation exhilarated them. They *knew* there was no one else for miles.

That was correct so far as it went.

Foam hissed and sprayed as Paul applied the church key to the cans. Above and below them, the wind broke like waves on the rocks.

"Mavrakis, you're going to the university, right?" said Paul.

Steve nodded in the dim moonlight, added, "I guess so."

"What're you going to take?" said Ginger, snuggling close and burping slightly on her beer.

"I don't know; engineering, I guess. If you're a guy and in the college-bound program, you end up taking engineering. So I figure that's it."

Paul said, "What kind?"

"Don't know. Maybe aerospace. I'll move to Seattle and make spaceships."

"That's neat," said Ginger. "Like in *The Outer Limits*. I wish we could get that here."

"You ought to be getting into hydraulic engineering," said Paul. "Water's going to be really big business not too long from now."

"I don't think I want to stick around Wyoming."

Carroll had been silently staring out over the valley. She turned back toward Steve and her eyes were pools of darkness. "You're really going to leave?"

"Yeah."

"And never come back?"

"Why should I?" said Steve. "I've had all the fresh air and wide open spaces I can use for a lifetime. You know something? I've never even seen the ocean." And yet he had felt the ocean. He blinked. "I'm getting out."

"Me too," said Ginger. "I'm going to stay with my aunt and uncle in L.A. I think I can probably get into the University of Southern California journalism school."

"Got the money?"

"I'll get a scholarship."

"Aren't you leaving?" Steve said to Carroll.

"Maybe," she said. "Sometimes I think so, and then I'm not so sure."

"You'll come back even if you do leave," said Paul. "All of you'll come back."

"Says who?" Steve and Ginger said it almost simultaneously.

"The land gets into you," said Carroll. "Paul's dad says so."

"That's what he says." They all heard anger in Paul's voice. He opened another round of cans. Ginger tossed her empty away and it clattered down the rocks, a noise jarringly out of place.

"Don't," said Carroll. "We'll take the empties down in a sack."

"What's wrong?" said Ginger. "I mean, I . . ." Her voice trailed off and everyone was silent for a minute, two minutes, three.

"What about you, Paul?" said Carroll. "Where do you want to go? What do you want to do?"

"We talked about——" His voice sounded suddenly tightly

controlled. "Damn it, I don't know now. If I come back, it'll be with an atomic bomb—"

"What?" said Ginger.

Paul smiled. At least Steve could see white teeth gleaming in the night. "As for what I want to do—" He leaned forward and whispered in Carroll's ear.

She said, "Jesus, Paul! We've got witnesses."

"What?" Ginger said again.

"Don't even ask you don't want to know." She made it one continuous sentence. Her teeth also were visible in the near-darkness. "Try that and I've got a mind to goodnight you the hard way."

"What're you talking about?" said Ginger.

Paul laughed. "Her grandmother."

"Charlie Goodnight was a big rancher around the end of the century," Carroll said. "He trailed a lot of cattle up from Texas. Trouble was, a lot of his expensive bulls weren't making out so well. Their testicles—"

"Balls," said Paul.

"—kept dragging on the ground," she continued. "The bulls got torn up and infected. So Charlie Goodnight started getting his bulls ready for the overland trip with some amateur surgery. He'd cut into the scrotum and shove the balls up into the bull. Then he'd stitch up the sack and there'd be no problem with high-centering. That's called goodnighting."

"See," said Paul. "There are ways to beat the land."

Carroll said, " 'You do what you've got to.' That's a quote from my father. Good pioneer stock."

"But not to me." Paul pulled her close and kissed her.

"Maybe we ought to explore the mountain a little," said Ginger to Steve. "You want to come with me?" She stared at Steve who was gawking at the sky as the moonlight suddenly vanished like a light switching off.

"Oh my God."

"What's wrong?" she said to the shrouded figure.

"I don't know—I mean, nothing, I guess." The moon appeared again. "Was that a cloud?"

"I don't see a cloud," said Paul, gesturing at the broad belt of stars. "The night's clear."

"Maybe you saw a UFO," said Carroll, her voice light.

"You okay?" Ginger touched his face. "Jesus, you're shivering." She held him tightly.

Steve's words were almost too low to hear. "It swam across the moon."

"What did?"

"I'm cold too," said Carroll. "Let's go back down." Nobody argued. Ginger remembered to put the metal cans into a paper sack and tied it to her belt with a hair-ribbon. Steve didn't say anything more for a while, but the others all could hear his teeth chatter. When they were halfway down, the moon finally set beyond the valley rim. Farther on, Paul stepped on a loose patch of shale, slipped, cursed, began to slide beyond the lip of the sheer rock face. Carroll grabbed his arm and pulled him back.

"Thanks, Irene." His voice shook slightly, belying the tone of the words.

"Funny," she said.

"I don't get it," said Ginger.

Paul whistled a few bars of the song.

"Good night," said Carroll. "You do what you've got to."

"And I'm grateful for that." Paul took a deep breath. "Let's get down to the car."

When they were on the winding road and driving back toward Fremont, Ginger said, "What did you see up there, Steve?"

"Nothing. I guess I just remembered a dream."

"Some dream." She touched his shoulder. "You're still cold."

Carroll said, "So am I."

Paul took his right hand off the wheel to cover her hand. "We all are."

"I feel all right." Ginger sounded puzzled.

All the way into town, Steve felt he had drowned.

The Amble Inn in Thermopolis was built in the shadow of Round Top Mountain. On the slope above the Inn, huge letters formed from whitewashed stones proclaimed: WORLD'S LARGEST MINERAL HOT SPRING. Whether at night or noon, the inscription invariably reminded Steve of the Hollywood Sign. Early in his return from California, he realized the futility of jumping off the second letter "O." The stones were laid flush with the steep pitch of the ground. Would-be suicides could only roll down the hill until they collided with the log side of the Inn.

On Friday and Saturday nights, the parking lot of the Amble Inn was filled almost exclusively with four-wheel-drive vehicles and conventional pickups. Most of them had black-enameled gun racks up in the rear window behind the seat. Steve's Chevy had a rack, but that was because he had bought the truck used. He had considered buying a toy rifle, one that shot caps or rubber darts, at a Penney's Christmas catalog sale. But like so many other projects, he never seemed to get around to it.

Tonight was the first Saturday night in June and Steve had money in his pocket from the paycheck he had cashed at Safeway. He had no reason to celebrate; but then he had no reason not to celebrate. So a little after nine he went to the Amble Inn to drink tequila hookers and listen to the music.

The Inn was uncharacteristically crowded for so early in the evening, but Steve secured a small table close to the dance floor when a guy threw up and his girl had to take him home. Dancing couples covered the floor though the headline act, The Radford & Lewis Band, wouldn't be on until eleven. The warmup group was a Montana band called the Great Falls Dead. They had more enthusiasm than talent, but they had the crowd dancing.

Steve threw down the shots, sucked limes, licked the salt, intermittently tapped his hand on the table to the music, and felt vaguely melancholy. Smoke drifted around him, almost as thick as the special-effects fog in a bad horror movie. The Inn's dance floor was in a dim, domed room lined with rough pine.

He suddenly stared, puzzled by a flash of near-recognition. He had been watching one dancer in particular, a tall woman with curly raven hair, who had danced with a succession of cowboys. When he looked at her face, he thought he saw someone familiar. When he looked at her body, he wondered whether she wore underwear beneath the wide-weave red knit dress.

The Great Falls Dead launched into "Good-hearted Woman" and the floor was instantly filled with dancers. Across the room, someone squealed, "Willieee!" This time the woman in red danced very close to Steve's table. Her high cheekbones looked hauntingly familiar. Her hair, he thought. If it were longer— She met his eyes and smiled at him.

The set ended, her partner drifted off toward the bar, but she remained standing beside his table. "Carroll?" he said. "*Carroll?*"

She stood there smiling, with right hand on hip. "I wondered when you'd figure it out."

Steve shoved his chair back and got up from the table. She moved very easily into his arms for a hug. "It's been a long time."

"It has."

"Fourteen years? Fifteen?"

"Something like that."

He asked her to sit at his table, and she did. She sipped a Campari-and-tonic as they talked. He switched to beer. The years unreeled. The Great Falls Dead pounded out a medley of country standards behind them.

". . . I never should have married, Steve. I was wrong for Paul. He was wrong for me."

". . . *thought* about getting married. I met a lot of women in Hollywood, but nothing ever seemed . . ."

". . . all the wrong reasons . . ."

". . . did end up in a few made-for-TV movies. Bad stuff. I was always cast as the assistant manager in a holdup scene, or got killed by the werewolf right near the beginning. I think there's something like ninety percent of all actors who are unemployed at any given moment, so I said . . ."

"You really came back here? How long ago?"

". . . to hell with it . . ."

"How long ago?"

". . . and sort of slunk back to Wyoming. I don't know. Several years ago. How long were you married, anyway?"

". . . a year more or less. What do you do here?"

". . . beer's getting warm. Think I'll get a pitcher . . ."

"What do you do here?"

". . . better cold. Not much. I get along. You . . ."

". . . lived in Taos for a time. Then Santa Fe. Bummed around the Southwest a lot. A friend got me into photography. Then I was sick for a while and that's when I tried painting . . ."

". . . landscapes of the Tetons to sell to tourists?"

"Hardly. A lot of landscapes, but trailer camps and oil fields and perspective vistas of I-80 across the Red Desert . . ."

"I tried taking pictures once . . . kept forgetting to load the camera."

". . . and then I ended up half-owner of a gallery called Good Stuff. My partner throws pots."

". . . must be dangerous. . ."

". . . located on Main Street in Lander . . ."

". . . going through. Think maybe I've seen it . . ."

"What do you do here?"

The comparative silence seemed to echo as the band ended its set. "Very little," said Steve. "I worked a while as a hand on the Two Bar. Spent some time being a roughneck in the fields up around Buffalo. I've got a pickup—do some short-hauling for local businessmen who don't want to hire a trucker. I ran a little pot. Basically I do whatever I can find. You know."

Carroll said, "Yes, I do know." The silence lengthened between them. Finally she said, "Why did you come back here? Was it because—"

"—because I'd failed?" Steve said, answering her hesitation. He looked at her steadily. "I thought about that a long time. I decided that I could fail anywhere, so I came back here." He shrugged. "I love it. I love the space."

"A lot of us have come back," Carroll said. "Ginger and Paul are here."

Steve was startled. He looked at the tables around them.

"Not tonight," said Carroll. "We'll see them tomorrow. They want to see you."

"Are you and Paul back—" he started to say.

She held up her palm. "Hardly. We're not exactly on the same wavelength. That's one thing that hasn't changed. He ended up being the sort of thing you thought you'd become."

Steve didn't remember what that was.

"Paul went to the School of Mines in Colorado. Now he's the chief exploratory geologist for Enerco."

"Not bad," said Steve.

"Not good," said Carroll. "He spent a decade in South America and the Middle East. Now he's come home. He wants to gut the state like a fish."

"Coal?"

"And oil. And uranium. And gas. Enerco's got its thumb in a lot of holes." Her voice had lowered, sounded angry. "Anyway, we *are* having a reunion tomorrow, of sorts. And Ginger will be there."

Steve poured out the last of the beer. "I thought for sure she'd be in California."

"Never made it," said Carroll. "Scholarships fell through. Parents said they wouldn't support her if she went back to the west coast—you know how 105% converted immigrants are. So Ginger went to school in Laramie and ended up with a degree in elementary education. She did marry a grad student in journalism. After the divorce five or six years later, she let him keep the kid."

Steve said, "So Ginger never got to be an ace reporter."

"Oh, she did. Now she's the best writer the *Salt Creek Gazette*'s got. Ginger's the darling of the environmental groups and the bane of the energy corporations."

"I'll be damned," he said. He accidentally knocked his glass off the table with his forearm. Reaching to retrieve the glass, he knocked over the empty pitcher.

"I think you're tired," Carroll said.

"I think you're right."

"You ought to go home and sack out." He nodded. "I don't want to drive all the way back to Lander tonight," Carroll said. "Have you got room for me?"

When they reached the small house Steve rented off Highway 170, Carroll grimaced at the heaps of dirty clothes making soft moraines in the living room. "I'll clear off the couch," she said. "I've got a sleeping bag in my car."

Steve hesitated a long several seconds and lightly touched her shoulders. "You don't have to sleep on the couch unless you want to. All those years ago . . . You know, all through high school I had a crush on you? I was too shy to say anything."

She smiled and allowed his hands to remain. "I thought you were pretty nice too. A little shy, but cute. Definitely an underachiever."

They remained standing, faces a few inches apart, for a while longer. "Well?" he said.

"It's been a lot of years," Carroll said. "I'll sleep on the couch."

Steve said disappointedly, "Not even out of charity?"

"Especially not for charity." She smiled. "But don't discount the future." She kissed him gently on the lips.

Steve slept soundly that night. He dreamed of sliding endlessly through a warm, fluid current. It was not a nightmare. Not even when he realized he had fins rather than hands and feet.

Morning brought rain.

When he awoke, the first thing Steve heard was the drumming of steady drizzle on the roof. The daylight outside the window was filtered gray by the sheets of water running down the pane. Steve leaned off the bed, picked up his watch from the floor, but it had stopped. He heard the sounds of someone moving in the living room and called, "Carroll? You up?"

Her voice was a soft contralto. "I am."

"What time is it?"

"Just after eight."

Steve started to get out of bed, but groaned and clasped the crown of his head with both hands. Carroll stood framed in the doorway and looked sympathetic. "What time's the reunion?" he said.

"When we get there. I called Paul a little earlier. He's tied up with some sort of meeting in Casper until late afternoon. He wants us to meet him in Shoshoni."

"What about Ginger?"

They both heard the knock on the front door. Carroll turned her head away from the bedroom, then looked back at Steve. "Right on cue," she said. "Ginger didn't want to wait until tonight." She started for the door, said back over her shoulder, "You might want to put on some clothes."

Steve pulled on his least filthy jeans and a sweatshirt labeled AMAX TOWN-LEAGUE VOLLEYBALL across the chest. He heard the front door open and close, and words murmured in his living room. When he exited the bedroom he found Carroll talking on the couch with a short blonde stranger who only slightly resembled the long-ago image he'd packed in his mind. Her hair was long and tied in a braid. Her gaze was direct and more inquisitive than he remembered.

She looked up at him and said, "I like the mustache. You look a hell of a lot better now than you ever did then."

"Except for the mustache," Steve said, "I could say the same."

The two women seemed amazed when Steve negotiated the disaster area that was the kitchen and extracted eggs and Chinese vegetables from the refrigerator. He served the huge omelet with toast and freshly brewed coffee in the living room. They all balanced plates on laps.

"Do you ever read the Gazoo?" said Ginger.

"Gazoo?"

"The *Salt Creek Gazette,*" said Carroll.

Steve said, "I don't read any papers."

"I just finished a piece on Paul's company," said Ginger.

"Enerco?" Steve refilled all their cups.

Ginger shook her head. "A wholly owned subsidiary called Native American Resources. Pretty clever, huh?" Steve looked blank. "Not a poor damned Indian in the whole operation. The name's strictly sham while the company's been picking up an incredible number of mineral leases on the reservation. Paul's been concentrating on an enormous new coal field his teams have mapped out. It makes up a substantial proportion of the reservation's best lands."

"Including some sacred sites," said Carroll.

"Nearly a million acres," said Ginger. "That's more than a thousand square miles."

"The land's never the same," said Carroll, "no matter how much goes into reclamation, no matter how tight the EPA says they are."

Steve looked from one to the other. "I may not read the papers," he said, "but no one's holding a gun to anyone else's head."

"Might as well be," said Ginger. "If the Native American Resources deal goes through, the mineral royalty payments to the tribes'll go up precipitously."

Steve spread his palms. "Isn't that good?"

Ginger shook her head vehemently. "It's economic blackmail to keep the tribes from developing their own resources at their own pace."

"Slogans," said Steve. "The country needs the energy. If the tribes don't have the investment capital—"

"They *would* if they weren't bought off with individual royalty payments."

"The tribes have a choice—"

"—with the prospect of immediate gain dangled in front of them by NAR."

"I can tell it's Sunday," said Steve, "even if I haven't been inside a church door in fifteen years. I'm being preached at."

"If you'd get off your ass and think," said Ginger, "nobody'd have to lecture you."

Steve grinned. "I don't think with my ass."

"Look," said Carroll. "It's stopped raining."

Ginger glared at Steve. He took advantage of Carroll's diversion and said, "Anyone for a walk?"

The air outside was cool and rain-washed. It soothed tempers. The trio walked through the fresh morning along the cottonwood-lined creek. Meadowlarks sang. The rain front had moved far to the east; the rest of the sky was bright blue.

"Hell of a country, isn't it?" said Steve.

"Not for much longer if——" Ginger began.

"Gin," Carroll said warningly.

They strolled for another hour, angling south where they could see the hills as soft as blanket folds. The tree-lined draws snaked like green veins down the hillsides. The earth, Steve thought, seemed gathered, somehow expectant.

"How's Danny?" Carroll said to Ginger.

"He's terrific. Kid wants to become an astronaut." A grin split her face. "Bob's letting me have him for August."

"Look at that," said Steve, pointing.

The women looked. "I don't see anything," said Ginger.

"Southeast," Steve said. "Right above the head of the canyon."

"There—I'm not sure." Carroll shaded her eyes. "I thought I saw something, but it was just a shadow."

"Are you both blind?" said Steve, astonished. "There was something in the air. It was dark and cigar-shaped. It was there when I pointed."

"Sorry," said Ginger, "didn't see a thing."

"Well, it *was* there," Steve said, disgruntled.

Carroll continued to stare off toward the pass. "I saw it too, but just for a second. I didn't see where it went."

"Damnedest thing. I don't think it was a plane. It just sort of cruised along, and then it was gone."

"All I saw was something blurry," Carroll said. "Maybe it was a UFO."

"Oh, you guys," Ginger said with an air of dawning comprehension. "Just like prom night, right? Just a joke."

Steve slowly shook his head. "I really saw something then, and I saw this now. This time Carroll saw it too." She nodded in agreement. He tasted salt.

The wind started to rise from the north, kicking up early spring weeds that had already died and begun to dry.

"I'm getting cold," said Ginger. "Let's go back to the house."

"Steve," said Carroll, "you're shaking."

They hurried him back across the land.

PHOSPHORIC FORMATION
PERMIAN
225-270 MILLION YEARS

They rested for a while at the house; drank coffee and talked of the past, of what had happened and what had not. Then Carroll suggested they leave for the reunion. After a small confusion, Ginger rolled up the windows and locked her Saab and Carroll locked her Pinto.

"I hate having to do this," said Carroll.

"There's no choice any more," Steve said. "Too many people around now who don't know the rules."

The three of them got into Steve's pickup. In fifteen minutes they had traversed the doglegs of U.S. 20 through Thermopolis and crossed the Big Horn River. They passed the massive mobile home park with its trailers and RV's sprawling in carapaced glitter.

The flood of hot June sunshine washed over them as they passed between the twin bluffs, red with iron, and descended into the miles and years of canyon.

TENSLEEP FORMATION
PENNSYLVANIAN
270-310 MILLION YEARS

On both sides of the canyon, the rock layers lay stacked like sections from a giant meat slicer. In the pickup cab, the passengers had been listening to the news on KTWO. As the canyon deepened, the reception faded until only a trickle of static came from the speaker. Carroll clicked the radio off.

"They're screwed," said Ginger.

"Not necessarily." Carroll, riding shotgun, stared out the window at the slopes of flowers the same color as the bluffs. "The BIA's still got hearings. There'll be another tribal vote."

Ginger said again, "They're screwed. Money doesn't just talk—it makes obscene phone calls, you know? Paul's got this one bagged. You know Paul—I know him just about as well. Son of a bitch."

"Sorry there's no music," said Steve. "Tape player busted a while back and I've never fixed it."

They ignored him. "Damn it," said Ginger. "It took almost fifteen years, but I've learned to love this country."

"I know that," said Carroll.

No one said anything for a while. Steve glanced to his right and saw tears running down Ginger's cheeks. She glared back at him defiantly. "There's Kleenexes in the glove box," he said.

MADISON FORMATION
MISSISSIPPIAN
310-350 MILLION YEARS

The slopes of the canyon became more heavily forested. The walls were all shades of green, deeper green where the runoff had found channels. Steve felt time collect in the great gash in the earth, press inward.

"I don't feel so hot," said Ginger.

"Want to stop for a minute?"

She nodded and put her hand over her mouth.

Steve pulled the pickup over across both lanes. The Chevy skidded slightly as it stopped on the graveled turnout. Steve turned off the key and in the sudden silence they heard only the light wind and the tickings as the Chevy's engine cooled.

"Excuse me," said Ginger. They all got out of the cab. Ginger quickly moved through the Canadian thistles and the currant bushes and into the trees beyond. Steve and Carroll heard her throwing up.

"She had an affair with Paul," Carroll said casually. "Not too long ago. He's an extremely attractive man." Steve said nothing. "Ginger ended it. She still feels the tension." Carroll strolled over to the side of the thistle patch and hunkered down. "Look at this."

Steve realized how complex the ground cover was. Like the rock cliffs, it was layered. At first he saw among the sunflowers and dead dandelions only the wild sweetpeas with their blue blossoms like spades with the edges curled inward.

"Look closer," said Carroll.

Steve saw the hundreds of tiny purple moths swooping and swarming only inches from the earth. The creatures were the same color as the low purple blooms he couldn't identify. Intermixed were white, bell-shaped blossoms with leaves that looked like primeval ferns.

"It's like going back in time," said Carroll. "It's a whole nearly invisible world we never see."

The shadow crossed them with an almost subliminal flash, but they both looked up. Between them and the sun had been the wings of a large bird. It circled in a tight orbit, banking steeply when it approached the canyon wall. The creature's belly was dirty white, muting to an almost-black on its back. It seemed to Steve that the bird's eye was fixed on them. The eye was a dull black, like unpolished obsidian.

"That's one I've never seen," said Carroll. "What is it?"

"I don't know. The wingspread's got to be close to ten feet. The markings are strange. Maybe it's a hawk? An eagle?"

The bird's beak was heavy and blunt, curved slightly. As it circled, wings barely flexing to ride the thermals, the bird was eerily silent, pelagic, fish-like.

"What's it doing?" said Carroll.

"Watching us?" said Steve. He jumped as a hand touched his shoulder.

"Sorry," said Ginger. "I feel better now." She tilted her head back at the great circling bird. "I have a feeling our friend wants us to leave."

They left. The highway wound around a massive curtain of stone in which red splashed down through the strata like dinosaur blood. Around the curve, Steve swerved to miss a deer dead on the pavement—half a deer, rather. The animal's body had been truncated cleanly just in front of its haunches.

"Jesus," said Ginger. "What did that?"

"Must have been a truck," said Steve. "An eighteen-wheeler can really tear things up when it's barreling."

Carroll looked back toward the carcass and the sky beyond. "Maybe that's what our friend was protecting."

GROS VENTRE FORMATION
CAMBRIAN
500-600 MILLION YEARS

"You know, this was all under water once," said Steve. He was answered only with silence. "Just about all of Wyoming was covered with an ancient sea. That accounts for a lot of the coal." No one said anything. "I think it was called the Sundance Sea. You know, like in the Sundance Kid. Some Exxon geologist told me that in a bar."

He turned and looked at the two women. And stared. And turned back to the road blindly. And then stared at them again. It seemed to Steve that he was looking at a double exposure, or a triple exposure, or—he couldn't count all the overlays. He started to say something, but could not. He existed in a silence that was also stasis, the death of all motion. He could only see.

Carroll and Ginger faced straight ahead. They looked as they had earlier in the afternoon. They also looked as they had fifteen years before. Steve saw them *in process,* lines blurred. And Steve saw skin merge with feathers, and then scales. He saw gill openings appear, vanish, reappear on textured necks.

And then both of them turned to look at him. Their heads swiveled slowly, smoothly. Four reptilian eyes watched him, unblinking and incurious.

Steve wanted to look away.

The Chevy's tires whined on the level blacktop. The sign read:

SPEED ZONE AHEAD
35 MPH

"Are you awake?" said Ginger.

Steve shook his head to clear it. "Sure," he said. "You know that reverie you sometimes get into when you're driving? When you can drive miles without consciously thinking about it, and then suddenly you realize what's happened?"

Ginger nodded.

"That's what happened."

The highway passed between modest frame houses, gas stations, motels. They entered Shoshoni.

There was a brand new WELCOME TO SHOSHONI sign, as yet without bullet holes. The population figure had again been revised upward. "Want to bet on when they break another thousand?" said Carroll.

Ginger shook her head silently.

Steve pulled up to the stop sign. "Which way?"

Carroll said, "Go left."

"I think I've got it." Steve saw the half-ton truck with

the Enerco decal and NATIVE AMERICAN RESOURCES DIVISION labeled below that on the door. It was parked in front of the Yellowstone Drugstore. "Home of the world's greatest shakes and malts," said Steve. "Let's go."

The interior of the Yellowstone had always reminded him of nothing so much as an old-fashioned pharmacy blended with the interior of the cafe in *Bad Day at Black Rock*. They found Paul at a table near the fountain counter in the back. He was nursing a chocolate malted.

He looked up, smiled, said, "I've gained four pounds this afternoon. If you'd been any later, I'd probably have become diabetic."

Paul looked far older than Steve had expected. Ginger and Carroll both appeared older than they had been a decade and a half before, but Paul seemed to have aged thirty years in fifteen. The star quarterback's physique had gone a bit to pot. His face was creased with lines emphasized by the leathery curing of skin that has been exposed years to wind and hot sun. Paul's hair, black as coal, was streaked with *firn* lines of glacial white. His eyes, Steve thought, look tremendously old.

He greeted Steve with a warm handclasp. Carroll received a gentle hug and a kiss on the cheek. Ginger got a warm smile and a hello. The four of them sat down and the fountain-man came over. "Chocolate all around?" Paul said.

"Vanilla shake," said Ginger.

Steve sensed a tension at the table that seemed to go beyond dissolved marriages and terminated affairs. He wasn't sure what to say after all the years, but Paul saved him the trouble. Smiling and soft-spoken, Paul gently interrogated him.

So what have you been doing with yourself?

Really?

How did that work out?

That's too bad; then what?

What about afterward?
And you came back?
How about since?
What do you do now?

Paul sat back in the scrolled-wire ice cream parlor chair, still smiling, playing with the plastic straw. He tied knots in the straw and then untied them.

"Do you know," said Paul, "that this whole complicated reunion of the four of us is not a matter of chance?"

Steve studied the other man. Paul's smile faded to impassivity. "I'm not that paranoid," Steve said. "It didn't occur to me."

"It's a setup."

Steve considered that silently.

"It didn't take place until after I had tossed the yarrow stalks a considerable number of times," said Paul. His voice was wry. "I don't know what the official company policy on such irrational behavior is, but it seemed right under extraordinary circumstances. I told Carroll where she could likely find you and left the means of contact up to her."

The two women waited and watched silently. Carroll's expression was, Steve thought, one of concern. Ginger looked apprehensive. "So what is it?" he said. "What kind of game am I in?"

"It's no game," said Carroll quickly. "We need you."

"You know what I thought ever since I met you in Miss Gorman's class?" said Paul. "You're not a loser. You've just needed some—direction."

Steve said impatiently, "Come on."

"It's true." Paul set down the straw. "Why we need you is because you seem to see things most others can't see."

Time's predator hunts.

Years scatter before her like a school of minnows surprised. The rush of her passage causes eons to eddy. Wind sweeps

down the canyon with the roar of combers breaking on the sand. The moon, full and newly risen, exerts its tidal force.
Moonlight flashes on the slash of teeth.
She drives for the surface not out of rational decision. All blunt power embodied in smooth motion, she simply is what she is.

Steve sat without speaking. Finally he said vaguely, "Things."

"That's right. You see things. It's an ability."

"I don't know . . ."

"We think *we* do. We all remember that night after prom. And there were other times, back in school. None of us has seen you since we all played scatter-geese, but I've had the resources, through the corporation, to do some checking. The issue didn't come up until recently. In the last month, I've read your school records, Steve. I've read your psychiatric history."

"That must have taken some trouble," said Steve. "Should I feel flattered?"

"Tell him," said Ginger. "Tell him what this is all about."

"Yeah," said Steve. "Tell me."

For the first time in the conversation, Paul hesitated. "Okay," he finally said. "We're hunting a ghost in the Wind River Canyon."

"Say again?"

"That's perhaps poor terminology." Paul looked uncomfortable. "But what we're looking for is a presence, some sort of extranatural phenomenon."

"'Ghost' is a perfectly good word," said Carroll.

"Better start from the beginning," said Steve.

When Paul didn't answer immediately, Carroll said, "I know you don't read the papers. Ever listen to the radio?"

Steve shook his head. "Not much."

"About a month ago, an Enerco mineral survey party on the Wind River got the living daylights scared out of them."

"Leave out what they saw," said Paul. "I'd like to include a control factor."

"It wasn't just the Enerco people. Others have seen it, both Indians and Anglos. The consistency of the witnesses has been remarkable. If you haven't heard about this at the bars, Steve, you must have been asleep."

"I haven't been all that social for a while," said Steve. "I did hear that someone's trying to scare the oil and coal people off the reservation."

"Not someone," said Paul. "Some *thing*. I'm convinced of that now."

"A ghost," said Steve.

"A presence."

"There're rumors," said Carroll, "that the tribes have revived the Ghost Dance—"

"Just a few extremists," said Paul.

"—to conjure back an avenger from the past who will drive every white out of the county."

Steve knew of the Ghost Dance, had read of the Paiute mystic Wovoka who, in 1888, had claimed that in a vision the spirits had promised the return of the buffalo and the restoration to the Indians of their ancestral lands. The Plains tribes had danced assiduously the Ghost Dance to ensure this. Then in 1890 the U.S. government suppressed the final Sioux uprising and, except for a few scattered incidents, that was that. Discredited, Wovoka survived to die in the midst of the Great Depression.

"I have it on good authority," said Paul, "that the Ghost Dance was revived *after* the presence terrified the survey crew."

"That really doesn't matter," Carroll said. "Remember prom night? I've checked the newspaper morgues in Fremont and Lander and Riverton. There've been strange sightings for more than a century."

"That was then," said Paul. "The problem now is that the tribes are infinitely more restive, and my people are actually getting frightened to go out into the field." His voice took on a bemused tone. "Arab terrorists couldn't do it, civil wars didn't bother them, but a damned ghost is scaring the wits out of them—literally."

"Too bad," said Ginger. She did not sound regretful.

Steve looked at the three gathered around the table. He knew he did not understand all the details and nuances of the love and hate and trust and broken affections. "I can understand Paul's concern," he said. "But why the rest of you?"

The women exchanged glances. "One way or another," said Carroll, "we're all tied together. I think it includes you, Steve."

"Maybe," said Ginger soberly. "Maybe not. She's an artist. I'm a journalist. We've all got our reasons for wanting to know more about what's up there."

"In the past few years," said Carroll, "I've caught a tremendous amount of Wyoming in my paintings. Now I want to capture this too."

Conversation languished. The soda-fountain man looked as though he were unsure whether to solicit a new round of malteds.

"What now?" Steve said.

"If you'll agree," said Paul, "we're going to go back up into the Wind River Canyon to search."

"So what am I? Some sort of damned occult Geiger counter?"

Ginger said, "It's a nicer phrase than calling yourself bait."

"Jesus," Steve said. "That doesn't reassure me much." He looked from one to the next. "Control factor or not, give me some clue to what we're going to look for."

Everyone looked at Paul. Eventually he shrugged and said, "You know the Highway Department signs in the canyon?

The geological time chart you travel when you're driving U.S. 20?"

Steve nodded.

"We're looking for a relic of the ancient, inland sea."

After the sun sank in blood in the west, they drove north and watched dusk unfold into the splendor of the night sky.

"I'll always marvel at that," said Paul. "Do you know, you can see three times as many stars in the sky here as you can from any city?"

"It scares the tourists sometimes," said Carroll.

Ginger said, "It won't after a few more of those coal-fired generating plants are built."

Paul chuckled humorlessly. "I thought they were preferable to your nemesis, the nukes."

Ginger was sitting with Steve in the back seat of the Enerco truck. Her words were controlled and even. "There are alternatives to both those."

"Try supplying power to the rest of the country with them before the next century," Paul said. He braked suddenly as a jackrabbit darted into the bright cones of light. The rabbit made it across the road.

"Nobody actually *needs* air conditioners," said Ginger.

"I won't argue that point," Paul said. "You'll just have to argue with the reality of all the people who think they do."

Ginger lapsed into silence. Carroll said, "I suppose you should be congratulated for the tribal council vote today. We heard about it on the news."

"It's not binding," said Paul. "When it finally goes through, we hope it will whittle the fifty percent jobless rate on the reservation."

"It sure as hell won't!" Ginger burst out. "Higher mineral royalties mean more incentive not to have a career."

Paul laughed. "Are you blaming me for being the chicken, or the egg?"

No one answered him.

"I'm not a monster," he said.

"I don't think you are," said Steve.

"I know it puts me in a logical trap, but I think I'm doing the right thing."

"All right," said Ginger. "I won't take any easy shots. At least, I'll try."

From the back seat, Steve looked around his uneasy allies and hoped to hell that someone had brought aspirin. Carroll had aspirin in her handbag and Steve washed it down with beer from Paul's cooler.

GRANITE
PRE-CAMBRIAN
600+ MILLION YEARS

The moon had risen by now, a full, icy disc. The highway curved around a formation that looked like a vast, layered birthday cake. Cedar provided spectral candles.

"I've never believed in ghosts," said Steve. He caught the flicker of Paul's eyes in the rear-view mirror and knew the geologist was looking at him.

"There are ghosts," said Paul, "and there are ghosts. In spectroscopy, ghosts are false readings. In television, ghost images—"

"What about the kind that haunt houses?"

"In television," Paul continued, "a ghost is a reflected electronic image arriving at the antenna some interval after the desired wave."

"And are they into groans and chains?"

"Some people are better antennas than others, Steve."

Steve fell silent.

"There is a theory," said Paul, "that molecular structures,

no matter how altered by process, still retain some sort of 'memory' of their original form."

"Ghosts."

"If you like." He stared ahead at the highway and said, as if musing, "When an ancient organism becomes fossilized, even the DNA patterns that determine its structure are preserved in the stone."

GALLATIN FORMATION
CAMBRIAN
500-600 MILLION YEARS

Paul shifted into a lower gear as the half-ton began to climb one of the long, gradual grades. Streaming black smoke and bellowing like a great saurian lumbering into extinction, an eighteen-wheel semi with oil-field gear on its back passed them, forcing Paul part of the way onto the right shoulder. Trailing a dopplered call from its airhorn, the rig disappeared into the first of three short highway tunnels quarried out of the rock.

"One of yours?" said Ginger.

"Nope."

"Maybe he'll crash and burn."

"I'm sure he's just trying to make a living," said Paul mildly.

"Raping the land's a living?" said Ginger. "Cannibalizing the past is a living?"

"Shut up, Gin." Quietly, Carroll said, "Wyoming didn't do anything to your family, Paul. Whatever was done, people did it."

"The land gets into the people," said Paul.

"That isn't the only thing that defines them."

"This always has been a fruitless argument," said Paul. "It's a dead past."

"If the past is dead," Steve said, "then why are we driving up this cockamamie canyon?"

AMSDEN FORMATION
PENNSYLVANIAN
270-310 MILLION YEARS

Boysen Reservoir spread to their left, rippled surface glittering in the moonlight. The road hugged the eastern edge. Once the crimson taillights of the oil-field truck had disappeared in the distance, they encountered no other vehicle.

"Are we just going to drive up and down Twenty all night?" said Steve. "Who brought the plan?" He did not feel flippant, but he had to say something. He felt the burden of time.

"We'll go where the survey crew saw the presence," Paul said. "It's just a few more miles."

"And then?"

"Then we walk. It should be at least as interesting as our hike prom night."

Steve sensed that a lot of things were almost said by each of them at that point.

I didn't know then...

Nor do I know for sure yet.

I'm seeking...

What?

Time's flowed. I want to know where now, finally, to direct it.

"Who would have thought..." said Ginger.

Whatever was thought, nothing more was said.

The headlights picked out the reflective green-and-white Highway Department sign. "We're there," said Paul. "Somewhere on the right there ought to be a dirt access road."

SHARKTOOTH FORMATION
CRETACEOUS
100 MILLION YEARS

"Are we going to use a net?" said Steve. "Tranquilizer darts? What?"

"I don't think we can catch a ghost in a net," said Carroll.

"You catch a ghost in your soul."

A small smile curved Paul's lips. "Think of this as the Old West. We're only a scouting party. Once we observe whatever's up here, we'll figure out how to get rid of it."

"That won't be possible," said Carroll.

"Why do you say that?"

"I don't know," she said. "I just feel it."

"Woman's intuition?" He said it lightly.

"*My* intuition."

"Anything's possible," said Paul.

"If we really thought you could destroy it," said Ginger, "I doubt either of us would be up here with you."

Paul had stopped the truck to lock the front hubs into four-wheel drive. Now the vehicle clanked and lurched over rocks and across potholes eroded by the spring rain. The road twisted tortuously around series of barely graded switchbacks. Already they had climbed hundreds of feet above the canyon floor. They could see no lights anywhere below.

"Very scenic," said Steve. If he had wanted to, he could have reached out the right passenger's side window and touched the porous rock. Pine branches whispered along the paint on the left side.

"Thanks to Native American Resources," said Ginger, "this is the sort of country that'll go."

"For Christ's sake," said Paul, finally sounding angry. "I'm *not* the anti-Christ."

"I know that." Ginger's voice softened. "I've loved you, remember? Probably I still do. Is there no way?"

The geologist didn't answer.

"Paul?"

"We're just about there," he said. The grade moderated and he shifted into a higher gear.

"Paul—" Steve wasn't sure whether he actually said the word or not. He closed his eyes and saw glowing fires, opened them again and wasn't sure what he saw. He felt the past, vast and primeval, rush over him like a tide. It filled his nose and mouth, his lungs, his brain. It—

"Oh my God!"

Someone screamed.

"Let go!"

The headlight beams twitched crazily as the truck skidded toward the edge of a sheer dark drop. Both Paul and Carroll wrestled for the wheel. For an instant, Steve wondered whether both of them or, indeed, either of them were trying to turn the truck back from the dark.

Then he saw the great, bulky, streamlined form coasting over the slope toward them. He had the impression of smooth power, immense and inexorable. The dead stare from flat black eyes, each one inches across, fixed them like insects in amber.

"Paul!" Steve heard his own voice. He heard the word echo and then it was swallowed up by the crashing waves. He felt unreasoning terror, but more than that, he felt—awe. What he beheld was juxtaposed on this western canyon, but yet it was not out of place. *Genius loci,* guardian, the words hissed like the surf.

It swam toward them, impossibly gliding on powerful gray-black fins.

Brakes screamed. A tire blew out like a gunshot.

Steve watched its jaws open in front of the windshield; the snout pulling up and back, the lower jaw thrusting forward. The maw could have taken in a heifer. The teeth glared white in reflected light, white with serrated, razor edges. Its teeth were as large as shovel blades.

"Paul!"

The Enerco truck fishtailed a final time; then toppled sideways into the dark. It fell, caromed off something massive and unseen, and began to roll.

Steve had time for one thought. *Is it going to hurt?*

When the truck came to rest, it was upright. Steve groped toward the window and felt rough bark rather than glass. They were wedged against a pine.

The silence astonished him. That there was no fire astonished him. That he was alive— "Carroll?" he said. "Ginger? Paul?" For a moment, no one spoke.

"I'm here," said Carroll, muffled, from the front of the truck. "Paul's on top of me. Or somebody is. I can't tell."

"Oh God, I hurt," said Ginger from beside Steve. "My shoulder hurts."

"Can you move your arm?" said Steve.

"A little, but it hurts."

"Okay." Steve leaned forward across the front seat. He didn't feel anything like grating, broken bone-ends in himself. His fingers touched flesh. Some of it was sticky with fluid. Gently he pulled whom he assumed was Paul from Carroll beneath. She moaned and struggled upright.

"There should be a flashlight in the glove box," he said.

The darkness was almost complete. Steve could see only vague shapes inside the truck. When Carroll switched on the flashlight, they realized the truck was buried in thick, resilient brush. Carroll and Ginger stared back at him. Ginger looked as if she might be in shock. Paul slumped on the front seat. The angle of his neck was all wrong.

His eyes opened and he tried to focus. Then he said something. They couldn't understand him. Paul tried again. They made out, "Goodnight, Irene." Then he said, "Do what you have . . ." His eyes remained open, but all the life went out of them.

Steve and the women stared at one another as though they were accomplices. The moment crystallized and shattered. He braced himself as best he could and kicked with both feet at the rear door. The brush allowed the door to swing open one foot, then another. Carroll had her door open at almost the same time. It took another few minutes to get Ginger out. They left Paul in the truck.

They huddled on a naturally terraced ledge about halfway between the summit and the canyon floor. There was a roar and bright lights for a few minutes when a Burlington Northern freight came down the tracks on the other side of the river. It would have done no good to shout and wave their arms, so they didn't.

No one seemed to have broken any bones. Ginger's shoulder was apparently separated. Carroll had a nosebleed. Steve's head felt as though he'd been walloped with a two-by-four.

"It's not cold," he said. "If we have to, we can stay in the truck. No way we're going to get down at night. In the morning we can signal people on the road."

Ginger started to cry and they both held her. "I saw something," she said. "I couldn't tell—what was it?"

Steve hesitated. He had a hard time separating his dreams from Paul's theories. The two did not now seem mutually exclusive. He still heard the echoing thunder of ancient gulfs. "I'm guessing it's something that lived here a hundred million years ago," he finally said. "It lived in the inland sea and died here. The sea left, but it never did."

"A native . . ." Ginger said and trailed off. Steve touched her forehead; it felt feverish. "I finally saw," she said. "Now I'm a part of it." In a smaller voice, "Paul." Starting awake like a child from a nightmare, "Paul?"

"He's—all right now," said Carroll, her even tone plainly forced.

"No, he's not," said Ginger. "He's not." She was silent for a time. "He's dead." Tears streamed down her face. "It won't really stop the coal leases, will it?"

"Probably not."

"Politics," Ginger said wanly. "Politics and death. What

the hell difference does any of it make now?"

No one answered her.

Steve turned toward the truck in the brush. He suddenly remembered from his childhood how he had hoped everyone he knew, everyone he loved, would live forever. He hadn't wanted change. He hadn't wanted to recognize time. He remembered the split-second image of Paul and Carroll struggling to control the wheel. "The land," he said, feeling the sorrow. "It doesn't forgive."

"That's not true." Carroll slowly shook her head. "The land just *is*. The land doesn't care."

"I care," said Steve.

Amazingly, Ginger started to go to sleep. They laid her down gently on the precipice, covered her with Steve's jacket, and cradled her head, stroking her hair. "Look," she said. "Look." As the moon illuminated the glowing sea.

Far below them, a fin broke the dark surface of the forest.

THE END

EDWARD BRYANT wrote the book. Although born in New York, Bryant grew up on a cattle ranch at the foot of the Sybille Canyon between Laramie and Wheatland, Wyoming. He graduated from Wheatland High School in 1963 and then attended the University of Wyoming as a General Motors Scholar. Since 1969, Bryant has worked full-time as a free-lance writer, producing six books, two screenplays, and scores of short stories and articles. He has also worked as an artist-in-residence for the Wyoming Council on the Arts and other sponsoring bodies. In both 1979 and 1980 he received the Nebula Award of the Science Fiction Writers of America for the best short story of the year.

MICHAEL McCLURE illustrated the book. For six years, McClure was a news photographer for United Press International. He then worked two more years in the photographic department of the *Detroit Free Press.* Now he freelances from his home in Atlantic City, Wyoming. McClure has done projects for the Wyoming State Energy Conservation Office and was the photographer for the Wyoming State Land Use Plan.

ROBERT RORIPAUGH introduced the book. Having been both a rancher and a soldier, Roripaugh is now professor of English at the University of Wyoming, teaching creative writing and Western American literature. His novel, *A Fever for Living,* was published by William Morrow and Company in 1961. A second novel, *Honor Thy Father,* received the Western Heritage Award from the National Cowboy Hall of Fame as the Outstanding Western Novel of 1963. In 1976, Spirit Mound Press published his poetry collection, *Learn To Love the Haze.*

This first edition of
Wyoming Sun
was designed and typeset
at the Rue Morgue Press, Boulder, Colorado.
Text type is 11 point Baskerville.
Printed on 60 pound Warren's Old Style
by Thomson-Shore, Dexter, Michigan.

Of the 2,250 copies
250 are clothbound,
signed and numbered by the author.